A story created by Joel Conrad
and illustrated by Laura Conrad

ISBN 978-1-3999-3338-4

Story by Joel Conrad
Illustrations by Laura Conrad
Editing by Kyle Phaneuf
Layout by Taj Mihelich
Published by Joel Conrad

This is dedicated to Jessica, who is a bit of a wizardess herself, working her magic in her fight for justice. And to Ron, Laura's husband, a wizard when it comes to love.

This book began about 25 years ago when I was visiting my sister Laura and she was showing me some of the artwork she had been doing. In amongst this was a flyer or leaflet for the art club she belonged to in Milford, Michigan. I think this was advertising a show they were putting on or something but what grabbed me was a little drawing of a girl or young woman who was wearing a long dress with a pattern of astronomical figures--comets, stars, planets, that kind of thing. She wore a conical shaped hat made of the same material and she brandished a wand.

"What's with the little 'wizardess'?" I asked. Laura said she didn't know, it just came to her and she thought it looked good on the leaflet. I agreed. "I could write a story about that" I said.

The idea stuck with me. My daughter Jessica was about 11 years old then. I imagined the wizardess to be a few years older than her and someone Jessica would like and look up to. On the plane back to England, I thought about it a lot and before I knew it, I had the outline of a story.

When I got home, I started writing whenever I got the time and space, which isn't very often when you have 3 small children, 2 jobs, a hardworking wife, a house to look after, etc.

Eventually I was able to send a draft to Laura. She liked it and began sketching scenes from the story. I kept working on the text and this went on for a few years until we thought we had something worth reading.

Laura took on the job of getting it published. She had no idea how to do this. I was no help. She looked into this every now and then over the next few years. Other matters came up for both of us, other projects, life events, new jobs and so on. The book sat in a drawer. Like they do.

A few years ago, Laura explained that she had been talking to an agent who thought we had something. The agent suggested adding some more illustrations and Laura had been working on them. Then Laura got sick and the illness meant she would never be able to continue her artwork.

This book is our way of getting the story with Laura's lovely drawings between covers and in her hands.

I say 'our' way as I couldn't have done this on my own. Fortunately, Laura was smart enough to have two smart sons. Kyle is a writer and has experience of editing and Taj is a graphic artist who has self-published. Together we pulled the book out of the drawer.

I hope you enjoy it. I hope Jessica likes it. And I really hope Laura does.

-Joel

Jescinta
Wizardess of Canabria

Dawn

As usual, Jescinta woke to the morning's first bird song. Sitting up in her little petal-and-down bed, she stretched, yawned, and looked out of the small window. She could see a slight lightening in the eastern sky, although it was still dark in her tree-home. She spent a few moments remembering her dreams. Then she swung out of bed, stretched again, and twirled on her toes.

Feeling her way across the room, she reached the wall where her wand hung. She found it and took it off its hook. She removed the wand's cover and its soft light gently filled the room. The handle was a stout stick of yew and at the end was fastened a special crystal. It drank in greedily the growing light of the dawn that eased through the window and the crystal grew a little brighter. As more and more birds woke and joined in the morning song, she thought for a moment about what she wanted to do on this day.

There were some herbs in her garden that needed gathering, she wanted to look for mushrooms, a swim would be nice, and she wanted to spend some time on that new remedy for warts that she had been working on.

She looked around her little room. She could see it more clearly now with the lights of her wand and the dawn growing stronger.

Jescinta noted the jars and pots waiting on their shelves, the big work table, her wardrobe, and all her things hanging and waiting here and there as she'd left them. Looking at the kitchen area, she thought of breakfast.

After a quick bowl of grains, nuts and fruit in doe's milk, she changed into a little shift, grabbed her wand, and climbed the stairs to the attic. Passing the bundles of cattails hanging in the attic, she remembered that she needed to make flour.

She pushed open the little door and stepped out into the morning.

From the lowest branch of her tree-home, she peered through the glum light at the forest spreading all around her. There was a rustle in the fallen leaves on the ground and a stirring in the branches all around as more and more birds woke and added their voice to the growing dawn chorus.

There was a slight swish of air and she turned to see her advisor and dear friend, the owl Oo-oo-luf, land on the branch near the attic doorway.

"Good morning, my friend," she said.

"And a good morning to you, mistress Jescinta," the owl replied. "I hope you slept well."

"Oh thank you, I did. I had such funny dreams. And how was your night?"

"Very nice, thank you. Several fluffy mice joined me for dinner and now I feel well fed and sleepy."

"I will leave you to it then and I hope you rest well," the little wizardess replied. The owl disappeared through the doorway to begin his day's sleep while Jescinta scampered up the rope ladder to the next branch. She nimbly picked her way up branches and steps, ropes, and ladders she had made until she finally came to the top of her tree.

Jescinta's home was a giant, ancient oak—the oldest creature in the forest. It stood in the middle of a broad, wooded valley that stretched to mountains circling all around. The great oak was the sole survivor of a terrible fire that ravaged the valley a very long time ago. The tree still held the sadness of the fiery end of its neighbors in its heavy, sagging limbs. The flames had eaten a hole deep into its trunk, providing, some ages later, a comfortable living quarters for the young wizardess.

When Goddell, Jescinta's wizard master had first showed her the old tree and said that this was to be her home while she was wizardess of this region of Canabria, she was thrilled and loved the oak like a friend from the start.

Settling into a crook of the highest branch, she looked at the dawn sky all around her. She positioned herself facing the east where the thin crimson line of the sun was creeping into view over the mountains. Above and behind her to the west, where the sky was still dark, the stars twinkled their last before they began their day's sleep. Placing her wand's crystal against her forehead, Jecinta closed her eyes and opened her mind to welcome the new day.

Chapter 2

A Messenger

Noon of the first day of Jescinta's first great adventure as the Wizardess of Canabria found her sunning herself on a broad flat rock at the base of a small waterfall. After completing her morning chores, she had followed the little creek that ran near her home, wading and rock-hopping and gathering what precious and useful things she could find. She had now in her shoulder bag seven nuggets of gold, a small diamond, a piece of driftwood shaped like a crescent moon, some mandrake, and a collection of mushrooms and toadstools. She had several times slid down the rocky shoot of the waterfall and swam in the pool at its base and now she rested and let the sun dry her.

She was startled from her reveries by a flapping of huge wings as a great heron landed on the rock next to her. The bird studied her for a moment before speaking.

"Good day to you, mistress Jescinta. Forgive me if I have given you a fright, I did not wish to do so."

Jescinta was taken aback by being addressed by the bird. However many times she met animals with whom she could communicate, she was and always would be filled with awe that it was possible. It was her special gift that she could talk with animals and it was this gift that led her to the attention of Goddell and eventually to being a wizardess. She would speak in her normal voice and they would speak in their usual way and somehow, sometimes, they would understand each other. She couldn't speak with every animal, only certain ones—usually leaders of their kind. Even then there were times when she could not make herself understood, such as when they were very frightened or when they were in a killing mind.

"Well, yes you did give me a bit of a fright, but that's all right," she replied when she had gathered her wits. "It's very nice to meet you, Mr..."

"Blue, they call me Blue. And it is a pleasure indeed to meet you, mistress," the heron replied nobly. "I have heard such a great deal about you—we all have. We welcome you to Canabria."

"Thank you, Blue. And to what do I owe the pleasure of this visit? Have you simply come to make my acquaintance and bring me greetings from your friends?"

"I fear not, mistress," he answered sadly, reluctantly. "I have come from the region of Allsworthy with bad tidings. All is not as it should be there and we fear it cannot be put right without your doing.”

“Oh dear, please tell me what this trouble is!” Jescinta requested, sitting up alertly.

“Human trouble … the worst kind!” Blue answered bitterly. “They are a strange and terrible lot,” he continued until he remembered to whom he spoke before he apologized. “Forgive me, I mean no offense, mistress Jescinta.”

“None taken, Blue. You are right, humans can be difficult to understand and they can behave badly,” the girl said, trying to put her visitor at ease. “Please continue. Which humans are causing you trouble?”

“Strangers, mistress. The humans of Allsworthy we can tolerate … we have become used to their ways. But these newcomers are different. They have descended on our region in a great flock with their horses and weapons and hunting dogs. They have encircled the city’s castle and there they wait and while they wait they hunt mercilessly and fell the trees to make their war machines and feed their fires. All the creatures of Allsworthy live fearfully and even the frogs are wary, hiding in their holes so that even I struggle for a meal,” the heron complained.

“Who are these strangers and what brings them to Canabria?” Jescinta asked.

“We do not know who they are, mistress. We have not seen their like before. They are small with hair on their faces and wolf skins for cloaks. They have banners with a wolf head snarling. They are cruel and unhappy and they go everywhere on their horses, armed and ready to kill. The people of Allsworthy fear them as much as the frogs and those that have not died by their hands hide in the castle,” Blue answered.

Jescinta shuddered, realizing that an invading army was laying siege to the gentle city of Allsworthy in the far southern corner of her district of Canabria.

“Thank you for bringing me this news, friend Blue,” she said, trying to sound strong and grown-up as she rose to her feet. “I shall leave as soon as possible to do what I can. It will take me a few days to get to Allsworthy as I am not blessed with your mighty wings. But I shall fly as best I can. Take heart and assure your friends.”

“Thank you mistress Jescinta. You are as brave and wise as they say. We will await your arrival”, the heron replied, before bowing respectfully and launching into the air with graceful flaps of his huge wings.

Jescinta watched him turn south and disappear over the trees before she gathered her things and headed hurriedly home to prepare for her journey to Allsworthy.

Chapter 3

Visitors

As she picked her way back down the little creek toward her home, Jescinta thought—not for the first time—that she was too young to be a wizardess. The peace and well-being of a district as large as Canabria was a heavy burden for such small shoulders. She recalled the events that had led to her being in this difficult position. She felt again, as fresh as ever, the terrible pain of the death of her parents from plague when she could barely walk. She remembered her bewilderment at being taken in by the village midwife and, eventually, the security and happiness she found living in the home of the old, kind woman. She thought again about the woman's amazed response when she saw her little charge talking to a cat and the animal doing exactly as the child asked. Jescinta remembered the long walk into the mountains at the old midwife's side to the home of the master wizard Goddell, and their farewells before the good woman returned home alone. She had been frightened by Goddell at first, and who wouldn't have been? But gradually she became convinced of his kindness and she took pleasure in his company and her chores as his assistant. She recalled her initiation at the Gathering of the Wizards, the challenge of their questions and tests, the thrill of their acceptance of her and, shortly afterwards, her journey with Goddell to her new home responsibilities as Wizardess of Canabria.

As Jescinta drew near to her beloved oak, she tried to plan her preparations. What should she take? How long would she be gone? What will she do when she gets there? What will be the outcome? If only Goddell were there, he would know. She had not seen him since he had brought her to this splendid tree. He had promised to visit regularly but where was he when she needed him?

Hurrying through the heavy wooden door at the base of the oak, she took her under-waist coat from its hook and laid it upon the big work table.

She would wear it under her wizardess dress and its many pockets would hold the secret potions, powders, herbs, and such that is the wizard's stock and trade. From the many jars and pots that filled the shelves of her dwelling she took a little of this and that, placing each into vials and pouches which she tucked into the pockets of the under-waist coat. All this took great care and time and when she had finished, she realized that it was beginning to grow dark.

Just then, there was a scratching and heavy clawing at the door to her home. Jescinta hurried to undo the latch and a great shaggy hound burst through, its tail pounding the sides of the doorway as it entered before leaping to land its huge paws on her shoulders and slather her face with its long wet tongue.

"Beomutt!" Jescinta exclaimed, recognizing the great hound immediately. She threw her arms around his thick neck, thrilled to see her old friend again, then she guided him back to the ground before she collapsed under his weight and enthusiasm. "How wonderful to see you! How are you?" she enquired before she realized the full significance of this unexpected visitor. "Goddell! Is he with you?" she asked excitedly, knowing that where the hound traveled, the master would not be far behind.

The girl hurried to the doorway and peered through the evening's darkening light. Presently, a tall figure appeared. She rushed out the door and down the path to the towering wizard that approached. She hurtled into him, wrapping her arms around his waist and nearly knocking the master wizard off balance.

"Steady on!" Goddell exclaimed, laughing. "I have walked three days and nights without food or rest and I shall collapse if you don't find me a chair, a plate, and a goblet very soon!"

When she had met her master's requests, Jescinta sat across the table from the wizard, watching him in silence as he devoured the bread and honey she had prepared and quaffed the mead she had poured for him. With her eyes, she drank in greedily his long weathered face, his white hair and beard, his huge hands, and shining, green eyes. Beomutt claimed his place in front of her little fire where he laid curled up and farting and she loved even that.

When he had finished and wiped his beard clean with his sleeve, Goddell finally spoke. "So, my young wizardess, how goes it?"

Jescinta burst forth with all that she'd been dying to tell him, how she'd been so busy decorating her new home, tending the garden, exploring the region, making friends with the creatures that lived nearby and generally living happily.

"And, oh Goddell!" she exclaimed breathlessly. "You would have loved the magic I did the other day! I was out for a walk when I came to a field where a young farmer and his wife were ploughing. They were so poor that he was pulling the plough like a beast and she was guiding it. And she was pregnant, so big with her belly out like this. They didn't notice me, they were working so hard. Just then, a rabbit hopped out in front of me. I fixed him with my gaze and he froze while I sprinkled transforming dust on him, recited the spell and changed the rabbit into a beautiful plow horse. I led him into the field and hid. When the farmers turned their plow, panting and sweating from their labor, there was this wonderful horse waiting to do their work for them. You should have seen their faces! I had never done that kind of magic before and I wasn't sure I could."

"Ah, you did well. Your love of the farmers made you able to do your magic," Goddell commented.

"Yes, just as you always said it would, but I could never quite believe it until then," Jescinta replied. Then the girl's face darkened as she remembered the really big news she had for her master—the trouble in Allsworthy.

Goddell noted the sudden change in the girl, one moment smiling and shining and the next all gloom and worry. This open innocence reminded him that his charge was still very much a child. He asked Jescinta what troubled her and she told him about her visit from Blue. The wizard listened intently and when she had finished, he thought for a moment before speaking.

"Did Blue mention anything about a wizard?" he asked.

"No, he didn't. Why?"

"That will be the Horsacks," Goddell said, as if he had not heard Jescinta's question. "I had heard there was turmoil in their land and that they seemed intent on spreading the trouble. They live in the high plains beyond the mountains to the south of Canabria. They are a herding people when they are at peace but very fierce when they are at war. I hadn't realized they would get this far north so soon."

Jescinta stood up, suddenly feeling restless.

"I told Blue I would leave for Allsworthy right away," she explained. "I was packing when you arrived. I wasn't sure what to take."

"Well, I'd better let you get on with it. I too have far to go," Goddell said as he got up from the table. "Thank you for the feed. That was just what I needed."

Seeing his master preparing to go, Beomutt rose reluctantly from his place in front of the fire, stretched, wagged his tail feebly, and moved to Goddell's side.

"It was my pleasure," Jescinta replied. "It's so nice to see you both. Do you have to go this evening? You could stay here if you wanted to rest for the night. Where do you go?"

"Oh, no thank you. There are still a few miles in these old legs," Goddell said, seeming to not hear Jescinta's question. "Do you travel alone?"

"I imagine Oo-oo-luf will want to come," the girl explained. "I haven't told you about him. He's a funny little owl who lived in this tree when I arrived. He seems to have adopted me. He's full of advice ... some of it's good. And I have another friend—a stag, Urun—who has been very kind to me. I'm hoping he will carry me to Allsworthy."

"Good, it's good to have friends on a journey," Goddell said, his hand reaching out to scratch Beomutt's head as he spoke. He still marvelled at the girl's gift with animals and it takes a lot to make an old wizard marvel. He smiled to himself, remembering that she maintained that it was not she who was gifted but the animals, who could somehow communicate with a little girl.

He moved to the door and Jescinta stood with him a moment, her little hands in his.

"I wish you luck in your mission, Jescinta, Wizardess of Canabria. I'm sure you will do well," he said, his eyes showing both confidence and concern. In reply, Jescinta could only give his hands a little squeeze when really she had so much to say and ask. He gave her a warm smile and a hug before moving out of the door and into the darkening forest, calling over his shoulder, "Safe journey!"

"Safe journey," Jescinta managed to reply meekly, feeling very small and alone. She watched them until they passed out of sight before reluctantly pushing the door closed.

Chapter 4

The Journey Begins

Jescinta moved to the big work table where her under-waist coat lay with its many pockets filled with wizard secrets and she put it on over her tunic. Then she went to the wardrobe where she kept her wizardess dress.

She opened the doors slowly and a small smile of wonder and pleasure brightened her face as she beheld the beautiful dress. She wore it only on special occasions such as this and it always gave her so much joy. It was a gift from Goddell for her initiation into wizardom. She slipped it on over her head, smoothing the long skirt down over her legs, her hands thrilling to the smooth coolness of the material. She gave a twirl—the dress made her feel like that, billowing out as she spun. The cloth was of some fantastic design, shining and changing colors and patterns from time to time. Now it was a deep maroon with purple patterns of stars and other celestial bodies as if it was in a sombre mood.

She also took from the wardrobe her tall wizard hat, made of the same material as her wonderful dress, and she placed it upon her head. To complete the picture, she took from its peg her wand, removing its cover to expose its crystal tip. Then she stood before her long mirror.

'Not bad!', she had to admit to herself.

But the tall hat was impractical for travel so she put it in her bag, which she hung across her shoulders. Replacing the leather cover on the crystal, she draped the strap of her wand across her shoulders, too. Then she swung the big travel cloak over it all, pulling the hood up over her head. The cloak concealed her marvellous dress–anyone who saw it would know immediately that she was a wizardess and that was not always good.

She hurried up the ladder, through the attic and out of the little door onto the broad first branch of the oak tree. Taking the horn from her bag, she gave it a long blast, then another and then she waited. She sensed, rather than heard or saw, Oo-oo-luf alight upon the branch just above her.

"Ah, Oo-oo-luf, how are you?" she greeted the little owl.

"Hmm, hungry mostly. I was just about to breakfast with a very plump little vole when a loud hoot of a horn alerted the little morsel and a second hoot sent it scurrying into a hole in the ground," he complained.

"Oh, I'm sorry. That was my fault. I was calling Urun," she explained, showing the horn which she still held in her hand.

"I thought as much," the owl grumbled.

"I must leave tonight on a journey. I'll be gone for a few days at least."

"Allsworthy, perhaps?" he asked, enjoying the look of surprise on Jescinta's face. "I met Blue, an old friend of mine."

"So you know about the trouble there. I was wondering if you would like to go with us."

"You wondered if I would like to go with you? You make it sound like a day's outing to picnic among the bluebells, rather than a highly dangerous attempt to come between two armies of humans intent on slaughtering each other," Oo-oo-luf scoffed. He studied the girl and if he'd had eye brows, one would have been raised in gentle mockery. He sometimes thought that Jescinta was a mere fledgling and quite incapable without him. "Of course I am coming, mistress. I wouldn't think of missing the fun."

"Thank you, Oo-oo-luf. I don't know what I'd do without you." Jescinta replied. She knew the owl wasn't fully convinced of her capabilities yet. She wasn't that convinced herself and it was best to humour him.

They stood quietly on their perches, waiting. The sun's last light was quickly fading in the west and a waxing moon was just beginning to show itself in the east while through the branches and leaves of the forest the stars could be glimpsed to be gathering. Presently they heard approaching through the silence of the forest the heavy thudding of hooves upon the carpet of fallen leaves. When the great stag appeared below them, Jescinta dropped to the ground to greet him.

"Urun, how good of you to come. "

"Mistress Jescinta," the deer replied with a little bow of his head. "It is always a pleasure."

"How are you? And Deela, how is she?" she enquired of the stag's favourite doe.

"She is well, thank you, due any day now to give us another fawn," Urun replied.

"How exciting!" she said. "This is possibly a bad time for you, Urun, but I need to make a long journey and I'd hoped you would take me as there is some urgency to my mission. But I would understand if you felt you needed to stay with Deela."

"I am of no use to her now and besides, she has the rest of the herd to keep her company," he replied. "To Allsworthy, then?"

"So you, too, know of the trouble there?"

"Bad news travels fast," he said, bending his forelegs to make it easier for the girl to mount him. As Jescinta swung her leg over his thick shoulders and settled into position, he rose and started off at trot. He knew the way, all the secret paths and runs that crisscrossed the forest and moors. Jescinta thought how marvellous it was to travel by deer. She could feel his powerful muscles working beneath her and smell his strong musky odour. They would travel at night and sleep by day, as is the deer's habit, but they would proceed quickly and surely to the troubled city of Allsworthy.

Chapter 5

A Dangerous Rescue

They moved swiftly through the dark forest, the silence disturbed only by the thudding of Urun's hooves and the occasional scurrying of other night creatures keen to stay out of the stag's way. Oo-oo-luf made himself known from time to time, appearing perched on a branch overhead or breaking the quiet every now and then with a hoot. At that point in the night when the moon was high and bright, the peace of the sleeping forest was suddenly well and truly broken by a great roar of pain and rage.

Urun froze, his flared nostrils snorting the air to place the danger. Jescinta could feel beneath her legs his muscles tense and hairs bristle. Oo-oo-luf appeared on a nearby branch and the three travellers listened as the roars echoed around them.

"Come on," Jescinta ordered. "Let's see what the trouble is."

"Hm-uhm," Oo-oo-luf interrupted, nodding to the frightened deer. "Perhaps you and I could investigate on our own."

"Yes, of course," Jescinta said, realizing how un-deer-like it would be to go toward danger. "Urun, you wait here or move away a little, if you prefer, and I'll call you when it's safe."

On foot, the girl went toward the terrible noise while Oo-oo-luf flitted silently from branch to branch just ahead of her. Drawing very near the source of the disturbance, the girl slowly peeked around a tree to see a huge brown bear thrashing madly at the undergrowth, its forepaws swiping at saplings and sending them splintering to the ground, its fangs flashing in the moonlight and eyes wide with fear. She saw that one of its back feet was clamped in the steely grip of a large trap, leaving the flesh bloody and torn to the bone. The trap was secured by a strong chain to a stout stake driven into the ground, forcing the tortured creature to move around and around in a small circle of pain. Jescinta wanted to help the poor creature, but she knew that while the bear was in this state of pain, fear, and rage, she would never be able to talk with him even if he had the gift of communicating with humans. With no way to show her friendship, the bear would attack her as fiercely at the trees, bushes and air around him.

She thought for a moment and then retreated to a little rivulet she had passed. She began making a crude basket of twigs which she lined with a large leaf. Oo-oo-luf landed beside her.

"He seems a little upset," the owl observed as the bear's roars resounded all around them. "What have you got in mind?"

Jescinta didn't bother to answer, intent as she was on her preparations. She filled the makeshift bowl with water and then took a little pouch from an inner pocket. She didn't know how much of the powder to use. Her patient was pretty big and very aroused. She sprinkled in a lot and added a pinch for good measure. Then, using a knife, she cut away a slab of bark from a large pine, which she used as a plate to collect resin that oozed from the trunk. To this she added some ointment and powder from pockets of her under-waistcoat and she stirred the mixture with a twig. Then she spoke.

"Oo-oo-luf, do you think you could distract the poor bear for a moment so I can put this bowl of sleeping potion within its reach?"

"I can but try," the owl answered bravely.

Jescinta watched from behind a tree as Oo-oo-luf appeared on a branch just above the roaring bear. He hooted to attract attention and the bear stopped his miserable bellowing to focus on the small bird. Then he leapt up, his forepaws sweeping the air and his jaws snapping horribly. The chain held him back or else he'd have murdered the owl, who hovered flapping and screeching just out of reach. The girl hurried quietly forward, placed the bowl of water with its sleeping powder within the bear's reach and returned to her hiding place. Oo-oo-luf, seeing that he had done enough, flew out of sight. They waited. Eventually the bear found the bowl. His efforts to escape had left him dry. He sniffed the bowl and then lapped up its contents before resuming his demented raging. Jescinta feared she had not added enough of the sleeping powder, but was pleased to see the bear grow quiet, lie down and finally sleep.

She knew that the effects of the powder would not last long. She moved quickly but cautiously forward. Taking a strong stick, she pried open the trap, freeing the bear's torn leg from its ugly teeth. She spread the mixture of pine resin and healing ointment on the wound.

Suddenly, quicker than she had expected, the bear stirred. Before she could think what to do, the bear leapt staggering to his feet, knocking Jescinta to the ground. She fell face down and when she rolled over, she looked up to see the bear standing over her, his face just above hers. His drooling mouth was partly open, showing his huge fangs and lolling tongue. His eyes seemed to struggle to focus and his mouth came toward her. Jescinta closed her eyes, frozen with fear and prepared to die. In the time it takes for one last breath, there streaked before her eyes all that had passed to bring her to this final moment.

Instead of feeling the crunch of teeth crushing her skull, however, she felt the warm wet roughness of a huge tongue slathering her face. She opened her eyes to see the bear stumble over her and move unsteadily off into the forest.

Sitting up, Jescinta realized that at her moment of terror, she had wet herself. In her relief, she felt rising from within her an uncontrollable laughter that was soon shaking her shoulders and sending tears streaming down her cheeks. Oo-oo-luf landed at her side.

"Are you all right?" he asked, both concerned and disapproving.

The girl looked at the funny little bird with his serious, worried expression and burst out into even greater fits of laughter, shrieking and giggling, sending hysterical echoes bouncing around the sleepy forest.

Chapter 6

The Village of Despair

A drizzly dawn found the three travellers asleep in the shelter of a large beech tree. Urun lay curled in the crook of the roots at the base of the tree, his noble antlered head erect and big eyes closed. He had been relieved to hear Jescinta's horn signalling that it was safe to collect her and amused to hear the story of the dangerous rescue. The young wizardess lay curled up beside him, her cloak drawn tight around her to guard against the damp. Oo-oo-luf perched securely in a little hole in the tree's trunk, sleeping soundly if not a bit disgruntled as the night's adventures had left him little time to fill his ever present stomach. The rescue had left him even more uncertain of the young girl's competence and surer still of his own importance.

As usual, Jescinta awoke to the first bird song. Not wanting to bother the others and knowing they would sleep for the better part of the day, she got up quietly to have a little walk, as she did not know this part of the forest very well.

Her wandering took her to a human track, the sort she knew connected one village to another. She followed this for a ways, becoming aware of a strange, acrid smell. The track led from the woods out into open land where there should have been the crops of the village that lay ahead. Instead of green vegetables and golden grains, the fields had only blackened stubble, still smoldering in the light rain. As she approached the village, she saw that some of the buildings had also been destroyed by fire. The village seemed deserted. No dogs barked to warn of her approach and no humans came to greet her.

Drawing near the largest house, she could hear frightened voices, children crying and the moans of a man in great pain. She knocked firmly on the door.

The house fell quiet, except for the groans of agony. Presently, she heard a bolt sliding and locks clicking and the door opened a crack. A man stared at her, his fear giving way to surprise at finding a young girl before him.

"I am Jescinta, Wizardess of Canabria" she declared.

He showed even greater surprise before he slammed the door shut again. She heard hoarse whispers and soon the door opened again, wider, to reveal a tall woman wearing a bloodied apron. Her face, though tired and drawn, showed intelligence and authority.

"Welcome, mistress," the woman said. "I am Dolores, the village healer and this is the home of my brother Cyril, the headman. Please come in."

Entering, Jescinta saw the house crowded with people, some watching her vacantly while others hid their faces as they sobbed quietly. The wizardess nodded her greetings. She noticed one young tousled haired boy who eyed her intently with bright dark eyes. She smiled at him warmly and he beamed back at her.

"All the village is gathered here for safety," Dolores explained. "But I fear there is none in this wretched place."

Noticing the quiet moans of pain, Jescinta passed through the crowded room and entered a back bedroom, Dolores and the tousled haired boy following. There she found more people gathered around a bed where a man lay groaning in agony, his head and most of his body wrapped in dressings. Those parts of his flesh not yet covered had raw blackened burns. She moved to the bed and placed her hand on the man's bandaged forehead. In a firm voice she recited a prayer in a language the others could not understand and she continued to repeat the prayer, her voice growing and deepening each time.

"O agonus
du homme oo wales,
quom een moi corpus
a' tak moi sole!
O agonus
du homme oo wales,
sillic moi vanes
a' bern moi 'art!"

Her hand began to grow warm and then hot as the man's searing pain passed into her. It passed up her arm, causing her voice to quaver and her body to quiver. Soon her body was wracked and shaking with the man's burning agony, she moaned and shrieked, her eyes turning up into her head. The man fell quiet. With a great effort, the wizardess pulled her hand away and she moved trembling, pale and panting to a chair someone offered her. The man lay breathing peacefully at last.

When she had regained some of her strength, Jescinta looked to Dolores.

"Who did this?" she asked, nodding to the sleeping man, her anger showing in her voice.

"A dragon, mistress—he calls himself Malik. He descended on the village two days ago, demanding we send him, each day, a sacrifice of a child. He has destroyed our crops with his fiery breath to terrorize us into submission. Cyril, my brother," she explained, indicating the man on the bed, "stood up to the beast, saying we refused and Malik engulfed him in a ball of flame." Dolores shook and sobbed at the memory of the awful scene before continuing. "We have decided to give in. Peter, here, bravely volunteered to be the first."

Jescinta looked at the dark eyed, tousled haired boy Dolores called Peter and she smiled at him before reaching out to mess up his hair even further. She stood up then to discuss with Dolores how she intended to care for her brother, giving the healer some remedies and instructions in their use. Then she turned to Peter.

"So, my friend. You are expected by the dragon Malik. Do you know the way," she asked, her anger at the dragon's crime narrowing her eyes and squaring her shoulders. When the boy said he did she asked if he would take her there and when he answered yes again she ordered, "Then let us not keep this Malik waiting. Lead on!"

Peter led the way out into the drizzly morning and through blackened fields before turning onto a track that snaked its way up a steep hill where the burnt remains of trees smouldered. They came to the rocky outcrops at the top of the hill and the boy halted at the opening of a dark cave. Jescinta removed her shoulder bag and wand, giving them to Peter to hold. Then she took off her cloak and under-waistcoat, revealing her gown, now black with a pattern of orange and yellow fireballs and streaks of white lightning. From her bag she took out her wizardess hat, which she placed on her head, and then she had Peter return to her the wand. She removed its cover, giving it to the boy for safe keeping. The crystal barely glimmered in the dull light of the overcast morning.

"Peter," she said when she was ready to face Malik. "I want you to wait here. If I don't return, take these things you hold to Dolores. She'll know what to do with them."

Then she turned and entered the cave. The way led down steeply into the hill. Soon she had only the dim light of the wand's crystal to see by. The walls of the rocky passage dripped with slime and a foul stench assailed her nostrils as she descended further into the earth. The tunnel widened into a large cavern and she knew she was in the presence of the dragon. Stepping into the space, she could see the reclining shape of the gross reptile across from her and then the yellow of his half-opened eyes as he awoke at her approach. The cavern was hot and putrid with his breath.

"Well, well, the humans have sent me a girl," he said, his voice slow and croaky with sleep. As he spoke, little flames came from his huge mouth and flared nostrils, causing the crystal of Jescinta's wand to glow a little brighter. Now she could see more clearly the dark green of his awful shape. "How nice! And such a pretty girl," the dragon purred. "They have wrapped my present so nicely in such a lovely dress. That was thoughtful. Come closer, my little darling. Come to me."

Jescinta remained still, holding her wand aloft and staring grimly at the reptile. His eyes tried to hold hers, tried to entrance her with their soft yellow light. His voice crooned as he spoke and his forked tongue flickered invitingly.

"Come, my little precious, my sweetness, my morsel of innocence," he hissed, "Come to me!"

Jescinta nearly stepped forward, entranced by the soft, friendly voice of the reptile. His eyes held hers, drawing her towards him. Her body trembled strangely. But then she remembered the agony of the village headman, Cyril, and young Peter, who would have stood there before the hungry beast, and her anger returned and she stood still.

"Come, my little breakfast, I am ready, I want you now, the mighty Malik is waiting," he called. Seeing the girl fail to respond, he said in annoyance, "Very well, my shy bird, no doubt you are overawed by my presence. Never mind, little one, I shall have you. I shall have you my way. I shall have you toasted!"

With that, he opened his great mouth and blew a thundering ball of fire that rolled toward Jescinta. She covered her face with the sleeve of her wizardess dress and rocked back on her heels as the force of the flame hit her and passed on by. The wand's crystal drank in greedily the light of the fireball and glowed brightly. Her dress, now a pulsing pattern of orange and red, glowed.

Seeing his breakfast untoasted by his efforts, Malik merely smiled and cocked his head out of curiosity before sending another ball of fire at his victim. Again Jescinta shielded herself and again the crystal soaked up the light, becoming even more brilliant.

Looking somewhat flustered to see the girl still standing there staring at him so brazenly, Malik grew angry and he sent forth an even greater ball of flame and he was struck dumb to see that this had no more effect than his other efforts, except that now the rock at the end of the girl's stick glowed all the more brightly, causing him to blink. The girl's dress now displayed flashes of white and blue among the flickering orange and red flickering swirls. Malik began to think something was wrong.

"Who are you," he finally asked, panting heavily from his efforts.

Jescinta didn't bother to answer. Instead, she raised her wand which blazed fiercely, its searing light blinding the awful beast and forcing him to shut his eyes tight. When he opened them again, she was nowhere to be seen. Jescinta had retreated quickly back up the tunnel. Seeing the light of her wand in the tunnel, he gave a great roar and rose to charge after her. Before he could get out of his lair, Jescinta aimed her wand at the ceiling of the tunnel where it widened out into the cavern. A bolt of lightning thundered from the crystal, exploding into the rocks above and sending huge boulders crashing down. Again she pointed her wand at the ceiling, firing two more blasts into the rock. When the dust settled, she saw that the tunnel was sealed shut by a wall of granite, trapping the evil dragon Malik. He who would have eaten a child a day would instead now grow hungry in his foul, dark prison.

When she returned to the fresh air of the surface, she found Peter still waiting. She took her things from him and gave him a little bag of seeds and another of gold. She told him to give these to Dolores to help rebuild the village.

"Peter," she said. "You are bright and brave and we can expect great things from you. Thank you for coming with me to this hell hole and waiting so courageously. Go tell your people that the dragon Malik will bother them no more. I will return when my journey is over to see how you all fare."

Then the wizardess gave him a kiss on the cheek before she messed up his hair one last time. She stood and watched him skip joyfully down the hill, a precious bag in each hand.

Chapter 7

The Chase

Jescinta moved to the top of the burned out hill and found shelter from the rain among a jumble of rocks. She sat down to rest and think over the recent events; the trapped bear, the despairing village and its injured headman, the evil dragon. Weighing her thoughts, feelings and actions on these occasions, she wondered what it all said about the trials she had yet to face in Allsworthy and about her ability to meet them. It did not make her feel entirely confident.

She found herself remembering the long journey with Goddell from his home in the mountains to her new home in the great oak at the heart of Canabria. They had talked of many things during those days of walking through the wilderness and nights camping. She thought in particular about one evening when they had sat beside their little campfire after eating, each staring silently into the fire as tired trekkers do. She was full of misgivings and she finally felt she had to tell the great wizard about her fears.

"Goddell?"

"Yes?"

"You know, I'm not as big and strong as you."

"True."

"Nor am I as old as you."

"No. Thank you for reminding me."

"And I'm not as clever and wise, either."

"If you say so."

"Well, what I mean is," she tried to explain. "I'm not sure I'm up to being a wizardess. I am just a small, not very strong or clever girl. I don't think I can do it on my own."

Goddell looked up from the little fire to study the girl. His face showed nothing of what he was thinking.

"There is more to being a wizard than being big, strong, old and clever," he finally said, speaking slowly like he was explaining something again for the hundredth time. "A wizard must care for the creatures he or she serves without needing to live among them. The wizard must be able to live alone to practice magic, tend the garden, to meditate. The wizard must be brave, feel the wonder of creation, know good from evil, living for the first and loathing the other. The wizard must have the gift of magic, of course. They are born with it in their blood but it is of no use without this most important ingredient. The wizard must love. That is what gives their magic power. Anger and, even more, hate can also make magic, but that is not the way of the wizard." Goddell paused while he again studied the young girl before continuing. "You have all these things in greater abundance than most, precisely because you are not big, strong, old or clever. It is not for you or I to say whether or not you are up to being a wizardess, because you simply are."

Sitting atop the burned out hill, Jescinta remembered these words without fully understanding them. She knew that it was love that had made her draw out the pain from the injured village headman. Thinking this, she was reminded that the pain still lingered in her hand. However, it was not love but anger and maybe even hate in her magic when she trapped Malik in the cave. She was uncomfortable with having acted out of such dark feelings and she struggled to understand them. She grew tired of trying. She removed her wand's cover, placed the crystal against her forehead, closed her eyes and cleared her mind.

When she opened her eyes again, she saw that the sky had cleared and evening was drawing in. Taking the horn from her bag, she gave it two loud blasts to signal her companions.

Oo-oo-luf arrived first, alighting on her shoulder. He surveyed the scene before them—the smelly, smoking mouth of the cave, the blackened trees, burnt fields and smouldering village in the distance.

"Lovely," he said. "Simply charming. Whatever have you been up to?"

"I'll tell you later," Jescinta replied, smiling.

Urun arrived a little later, skittish about being in a place that still smelled of danger. They left quickly to spare the stag any further anxiety, heading south over rolling hills into moorland.

Dead of night found them on a high grassy hill where some ancient people had erected a solemn circle of standing stones. The moon hung in the sky like the watchful eye of a hungry cyclops. They stopped to rest and, while Urun grazed and Oo-oo-luf patiently waited for unwary mice from atop the tallest stone, Jescinta told them about the village and her battle with the dragon Malik.

"Well, I can see we're going to have to keep a closer eye on you in the future," the little owl said when she had finished her story. "If you are going to go off on your own like that looking for tr–"

He was cut short by a sharp yip yip that pierced the night, followed by an urgent yowl that echoed across the hills. It was a sound to freeze the heart of any creature unfortunate enough to hear it, the hunting call of the wolf. Urun's great head jerked up, his eyes wide with fright, ears straining, nostrils flared and snorting. As he stamped his feet and moved in a little circle, Jescinta leapt up, realizing that the stag was about to flee in a blind panic. She ran toward him and as she jumped onto his back, a second wolf howled and Urun was off. He leapt and bounded over rocks and down the hill, changing direction unexpectedly with each upward surge. The girl gripped tightly the long hair at the base of the deer's neck, her legs squeezing his sides, her hips trying to guess the direction of the next leap into the dark. She had ridden the stag before when he was in full flight, but that had been in fun and she had always eventually fallen off. This was different.

To her horror, Jescinta became aware of wolves closing in behind and racing along beside them. To her even greater horror, she realized that Urun in his mad, blind flight was careening down a hill and in the weird light of

the moon she could see that the hill ended abruptly at a steep ravine. A fall of several hundred feet awaited them if the wolves didn't get them first.

She reached inside her cloak, felt for a pocket in her under-waistcoat—she hoped it was the right one—and pulled out a little pouch. Somehow she managed to grab a pinch of powder from the bag, which she sprinkled on the head of the terrified deer. Then she quickly recited the spell:

Like a feather in the wind,
like a butterfly in the breeze,
let this creature walk
in the sky with ease.
Like a bird on the wing,
like a cloud in the sky,
let this creature who runs
know how to fly.

No sooner had she completed the spell than the stag took a desperate leap over a rock, the wolf pack gathering on either side. If the magic failed, his landing would take him to the exact edge of the cliff where he would surely stumble and the deer and his rider would fall to their death.

But the magic worked. Instead of ending at the edge of the ravine, Urun's jump took him high into the sky. His hooves clawed the air as they passed over the deep gorge. They landed on the other side with such force that Urun stumbled and Jescinta fell off, tumbling into a patch of gorse. The wolves watched helplessly from the far side as the stag careened breathlessly into the woods to safety.

Oo-oo-luf landed on a branch just above her. "Well, that was exciting," he crooned coolly, one big eye blinking slowly. His voice betrayed his amusement at seeing Jescinta sprawled among the gorse. "I hope you enjoyed your little gallop, mistress."

Chapter 8

Some New Friends and Allies

"Enjoy is not the word I would use to describe my feelings, Oo-oo-luf," the girl replied as she stood, straightening her clothes and pushing her hair from her face. She looked across the ravine to see the wolf pack turn away in search of other prey. "We will leave Urun to calm himself and lick his wounds while we go to find these wolves' lair. I would like to have a word with their leader."

"You want to go to the wolves' lair, mistress?" Oo-oo-luf asked, alarmed and confused. He could imagine nothing more foolish than going to the home of a gang of murderous carnivores.

"Yes, Oo-oo-luf," Jescinta replied. "I want to make sure this attack on Urun is not repeated. He must return to his home and Deela unharmed and our journey to Allsworthy must not be interrupted like this again."

With that, she began the perilous descent down into the ravine and up the other side. Oo-oo-luf made inquiries of animals he found going about their night business and after a fair journey they began to climb a hill known by all who lived nearby as Wolves' Tor. At dawn, they silently approached the top. Jescinta noted large holes dug beneath rocky outcrops, the dens of the wolf pack. At the top of the hill, they found the largest of the digs and there she waited. Oo-oo-luf perched on a high rock where he could see all around. For once he had nothing clever to say, instead his head just swivelled from side to side and his eyes stared even more widely than usual at the wolves' holes. He did not like this place and Jescinta could sense his fear.

Soon a little ball of white fur emerged from the wolf den. It stretched and yawned and looked around curiously. Suddenly the little she-wolf cub froze stiffly, her large pale blue eyes straining in the dim light to focus on the human shape that stood waiting before her. The pup's hair stood on end, her legs stiffened and tail stood upright.

Before the wolf cub could sound the alarm, Jescinta spoke to her.

"Hello, little one," she said softly, smiling and holding out her hand in friendship. The wolf cub cocked her head in surprise and her tail gave a couple uncertain wags. "Don't be afraid. I am a friend. My name is Jescinta. What's yours?"

The pup hesitated before answering. She was shocked at being spoken to by this human and confused as to what to do. Should she sound the alarm and bring out the pack or reply?

"Lupia," she decided to reply. "Princess Lupia."

"Lupia. What a beautiful name. It suits you," Jescinta said. "I have come to speak to the leader of this pack. Is he in?"

"Yes, Lupus, my father, King of Canabria," Lupia said proudly. "I'll get him."

Lupia turned back into the lair and a moment later she returned, followed by the powerful figure of the wolf-king, Lupus. Seeing the human, his yellow eyes narrowed, his ears folded back, the hair on his broad shoulders bristled and a low growl came from his deep chest. His lips curled, showing his huge fangs.

"Who dares waken me?" he demanded.

"I am Jescinta, Wizardess of Canabria," the girl replied, taken aback by his hostile manner.

Lupus did not relax his threatening stance as he studied the human who dared to trespass on his domain. Lupia, surprised by her father's aggressive response to the young girl she had thought was so friendly, became alarmed herself and moved to his side, copying his posture as best she could.

"And why have you come to Wolves' Tor, Wizardess?" Lupus finally asked, his tone showing clearly how little he cared for her title.

"Last night your pack attacked a friend of mine, the stag Urun. I've come to ask for your promise that it will not happen again," Jescinta replied in what she hoped was a firm voice.

"What? You come here demanding that wolves should not hunt as they please? How would you have wolves live? Like sheep or deer, grazing and chewing a cud?" he growled, disbelief and anger stiffening his body. "You call yourself Wizardess of Canabria. Do you know who I am? Lupus, King of Canabria! How large is your pack? How many hunters does a wizardess command? How many rivals have you defeated in combat to come to power? See my strength, wizardess, and then demand that I promise!"

With that, he gave three loud yips, the first in a high, shrill note that pierced the ear, the second lower and full of command, the third in a deep bass whose power rumbled like thunder.

Instantly wolves scrambled from their lairs all around and before she could think what to do, Jescinta found herself surrounded by the wolf pack, snarling and ready for the command to attack.

Jescinta struggled to hold back her fear. She fixed a firm eye on Lupus, who stood confident and waiting. When she spoke, her voice was sure and possessed an authority none could miss.

"Lupus, hear me out! I have not come to demand anything. I have come to your lair to ask a small favor of a great king. I ask that one deer should be left to travel in peace. There is plenty of other game for a pack as strong and swift as this. The stag Urun accompanies me on a mission of great importance to all of Canabria, including the wolves of this pack. The city of Allsworthy is under siege by an army of invaders from the south and if I am not allowed to travel freely to try to prevent the destruction of Allsworthy, the consequences for Canabria will be catastrophic."

Lupus listened to the girl intently and as he did so, his stance softened and he relaxed. He was struck by the confidence and command of her voice, soothed by her flattery and intrigued by her story. But he was not convinced.

"What do I care of the affairs of humans?" he asked. "They are fools. They kill out of madness and greed, rather than hunt only for food like honourable folk. It would be best if they were left to slaughter themselves so that other creatures could live in peace."

"It is true that humans do not always possess your wisdom, Lupus," Jescinta replied. "But the army that threatens Allsworthy is very powerful and they are likely to triumph. They are not like the humans you know. They are fierce and warlike. They fight and hunt on horseback. When they have conquered Allsworthy, they will spread their menace over all of Canabria. You should know what they feel about wolves. Their flags carry the symbol of a wolf head. Their war-cry is a howl you would be proud of. Their warriors wear wolfskins over their armour. When they have finished in Allsworthy, they will come here with their horses, dogs, and weapons and they will not rest until the coats of your pack are on their backs, you are a rug in their general's tent and the little princess here is stuffed with feathers and made a pillow for his bed."

Lupus shuddered at the scene the wizardess described. He looked around at his pack, who all watched him and waited for his decision. He looked down at his little princess, Lupia, who stared up at him, her fear showing in her wide, blue eyes. He was wolf-king not just because of his pride and strength but because he was also just, loving of his pack and wise.

"Tell the stag Urun he is safe from us. You may leave and travel in good speed and luck," he finally said. The wolf pack relaxed and broke the circle of threat around Jescinta. She went down to one knee and held out her hand to Lupia, who ran immediately forward, sniffed the offered hand and then licked the girl's face.

"Don't worry, little one. I will see that these things do not happen and that you and your pack can live in peace," Jescinta assured the wolf pup as scratched her ears and smoothed her silky coat.

"Yes, do that and when you have frightened off these horrible humans, come back and visit. I'll show you how to catch mice—I'm ever so good at that!" Lupia exclaimed.

"Oh, I'm sure you are, princess. I would love to visit you if I am allowed," the girl said, laughing and looking to Lupus. He nodded his approval and then said:

"Good luck on your mission, Jescinta, Wizardess of Canabria. You will always be welcome at Wolves' Tor. And if I can be of any assistance..."

Jescinta stood up and gave a little bow of gratitude to Lupus, Wolf-king of Canabria, before turning to descend Wolves' Tor and to resume her journey to the troubled city of Allsworthy.

Chapter 9

The Day Leads to a Knight

Mid morning found Jescinta approaching a small lake. Oo-oo-luf had flown on ahead and was probably sleeping soundly in a tree where nearby Urun dozed in some bower. Just as she was about to step out of the bushes onto the rocky beach of the lake, she froze. Ahead of her, a man kneeled naked on the stones at the water's edge. His body was erect and still, his hands pressed together, his head bowed and eyes closed. His hair was black and his face was smooth and calm. She noticed that the paleness of his strong body was lined here and there with scars of past wounds, some brown and old and some red and newer.

The beach stretched past him, nestling against the still water. The lake was as blue as the cloudless sky and as bright as the warming sun above. On the far side, the forest crowded close, reflecting dark greens and shadows into the water.

He opened his eyes and she saw that they were the same as the lake and the sky, as deep and still and blue. Jescinta's eyes drank in the scene and as she let out a long, slow sigh, she thought that probably she had never seen anything more beautiful than this moment by the lake.

Finally pulling her eyes away, she saw a ginger haired youth tying a bundle onto the back of a patient black oxen. A huge grey stallion grazed nearby and a small campfire warmed a pot.

The man rose now and paused for a moment before walking surely into the lake. When the water came to his waist, he stopped to splash and wash himself. Then he dived gently in, emerging with long, smooth strokes that sent him moving swiftly toward the lake's centre and little waves spreading slowly across the lake's calm.

When he reached the centre, he upturned and disappeared into the water without a splash. Soon the surface was smooth again, as if he had never been there. Jescinta waited for him to appear and she waited and waited. When she thought that now, surely, he would resurface but he did not, she began to think something was wrong. She looked over to where the young boy was brushing the stallion, apparently oblivious to the man's plight. Should she call out?

She looked back to the empty centre of the lake and just then he hit the surface. His right arm shot out first, piercing the sky, his hand held not in a fist but as if it gripped a sword. He gasped deeply as his head emerged and the force of his ascent took his torso above the surface before he sank slowly back down. Then he treaded water, looking around and breathing deeply, before he headed for the shore.

The boy met him there with a blanket and when he was well covered, Jescinta came out of her hiding and headed along the beach toward them. The man and boy watched her approach and when she drew near, she held out her hand in greeting.

"Good morning," she said a little louder than she had intended.

"A good morning to you, my lady," the man replied as he took her hand, bowing a little at the waist and smiling with eyes of lake and sky.

She turned to the boy and repeated her greeting. He did not speak as he stepped forward, but he took her hand eagerly and bowed deeply. His big green eyes and grin gave a warm hello.

"I don't wish to disturb you in your morning's preparations," Jescinta said. "I was passing this way and I wanted to make my greetings. My name is Jescinta."

"You are no disturbance, my lady, more a splendid surprise," the man said, smiling. "I am the knight Gawain and this is my squire Bartalemew." The boy beamed all the brighter. "Though you are passing and perhaps have some way to go, I do hope you can pause a bit and join us to break fast. If that is possible, Bartalemew will gladly attend to you while I, if I may, retire to dress." The boy nodded eagerly and Jescinta gratefully accepted.

Soon they were gathered around the small campfire, each with a bowl of porridge and a mug of hot tea, quickly prepared by the boy. Before eating, the man knelt as he had done beside the lake. The boy copied his master, watching the girl with one eye. Jescinta thought it might be rude not join them, so she knelt, too. The three were silent together, each with their own thoughts or prayers, until the man murmured a soft "Amen." The boy sat quickly down and began to eat eagerly. Gawain lowered himself slowly to the ground and waited for his guest to begin. Jescinta took a sip of her tea and she felt the man watching her.

"Tell me, Gawain, I can't hold my curiosity any longer, what brings you and your young squire to Canabria?"

"A dragon, my lady, a beast known as Malik. I have reason to believe he is in this district and I have come here for him. He is an evil creature who has caused much pain and fear. I have sworn to slay him," the knight answered gravely.

"Oh, Malik. Well, you needn't bother," she said, trying not smile. "I've already seen to him."

But she had to smile when she saw the surprise spread across the man's face and she had to laugh when she saw the boy's mouth fall open, overflowing with porridge. When she had composed herself, she told them of the village's despair and of her battle with the dragon in his cave. Gawain listened to all of this intently and he could not hide his wonder at what he heard.

"Forgive me, my lady, pray tell," he finally had to ask. "Who are you?"

Jescinta felt herself blushing. "Well, actually," she answered shyly. "I'm the wizardess around here."

There was a moment of silence as Jescinta watched their faces change into even more extreme looks of surprise. The boy had another huge mouthful of porridge that caused his cheeks to bulge. He made a little choking sound as he struggled to hold in the gloop in his gob. But he failed, spewing the lot into the fire in a big burst that sent exploding a small cloud of ash and a spray of embers. Gawain seemed not to notice. He stared at the girl with his head tilted queerly. One eyebrow was cocked halfway up his forehead while the other eye squinted in a hard stare and his mouth hung open slackly.

Jescinta felt a loud guffaw starting up in her belly. It rumbled up her throat and burst out in a loud shriek that made her rock back and clap her hands. She covered her mouth and fell hopelessly giggling.

"Oh dear!" she said when she was finally able to sit upright. "Oh dear, please forgive me. I mustn't laugh. Oh, it is rude. Aahmm, sorry, a...I'll explain. I guess you have some questions, but first, Gawain, may I ask, who are you?"

"Oh, yes my lady, a thousand pardons," Gawain said. "I now learn that we are guests in your...wizardom and to have not properly introduced myself and explained my business is a grave oversight. Forgive me. I am a knight of a distant kingdom. I am on a quest. I search for a holy relic that I hope to find and take back to my good King so that he may help to heal our nation's troubled soul. I have searched far and wide for many years, although it is fair to say that my progress has been sorely blighted by many interruptions. It seems that wherever I go I find trouble and strife, the weak against the strong, the bad troubling the good, the poor going without. And I cannot turn my back, I must pick a side and fight for the good. It was one such interruption that brought me here in pursuit of Malik. I have fought other such creatures and giant worms, witches, sorcerers, a giant, a troll, the lot. Not to mention the village whose well had run dry, homeless children, a swarm of locusts, the

Plague and such as that. To ignore such battles would be bad faith and not true to my quest. But I do fear at times that my quest may stay forever before me and I shall never find rest.”

"Oh I hope not, Gawain. I hope you find this relic and return to your home,” Jescinta said, noting the sadness in the man at the thought of his quest failing. “Who knows, maybe I can help. I hate to tell you this, having heard your plight, but I said I would tell you more and so I will. I am myself on a journey that involves the weak and the strong, the good and the apparently bad.”

She went on to tell him about the city of Allsworthy and its siege by the Horsacks. When he heard this, Gawain stood up and walked around the fire to Jescinta. As she rose to face him, he went down on one knee and bowed his head.

"My Lady Jescinta, Wizardess of Canabria, slayer of the dragon Malik, I, Sir Gawain, Knight of the Table, ask that you honor my humble request and allow me to swear allegiance to your cause and ride with you as your servant.”

Jescinta thought, ‘Well, what can I say?’ She loosened her cloak and let it slip to the ground. Her dress shimmered a deep azure with gold trim. She looked to Bartalemew, who tried to show her what to do by placing his hand atop his ginger head. Jescinta raised her right hand and she looked to see if it was clean before placing it on the warm, soft black hair of the head offered her.

"That’s very kind, Gawain. It would be very nice to have you along. Thank you.”

Chapter 10

The Knight's Story

The afternoon found Jescinta seated behind Gawain on the grey stallion as they moved along a friendly woodland trail. Bartalemew rode behind on the laden oxen, his legs straddling its thick neck.

"Gawain, please, tell me more about your quest," Jescinta asked.

"My lady, a pleasure," Gawain replied, smiling over his shoulder. "But to do so, I must do some explaining. From what little I know of you and your Canabria, I think you would guess little of where my quest came from. So, I must begin at the beginning.

"When I was a boy, my nation was at war with itself. Each prince, baron, duke, or earl saw his neighbor as a possible or an actual enemy. Every town or city was at war or planning war or busy defending themselves against attack. There was no one who could come forward and put the fighting to an end.

"My father was a landowner and had twenty men and their families to work the land. With the housemen and stable boys, he could raise a crack troupe of thirty cavalry when he needed. He pledged allegiance with a baron whose land neighboured his. They had known each other since boyhood and trusted each other like brothers. With the baron's strong castle and my father's horsemen, they made a formidable foe and we were left in relative peace by our more greedy neighbours.

"This baron had fostered a foundling, under circumstances of great secrecy. When he was still but a child, this ward of the baron declared himself king, by reason of having passed a sacred test. Many strong men opposed the boy-who-would-be-king, and he was forced to fight for his throne. My father, out of loyalty to his friend the baron, was one of those who threw in their lot with the young pretender to the throne. The boy proved to be a good general and his first few battles to gain his crown were won. Over the coming years, he gained in strength as one by one his foes fell. When I came of age, I became squire to his finest knight and then I, too, gained my knighthood. I was the youngest to sit at the King's table. The honour I felt at being in such exalted company as the King and his knights cannot be told. Soon the last battle was fought and the kingdom was secured. The King was crowned in a tremendous ceremony in the cathedral and we knights stood by his side.

"The nation now discovered a peace it had never known. Without the threat of war, the farmer could tend his crop, the painter his canvas, the builder his plans and the minstrel his song. During the long years of war, we knights had often talked of what we fought for, the peace we imagined, the nation we hoped to build. Under the King's direction, we began the building of roads, cathedrals and libraries and at times it looked like all our dreams might become true.

"But those who are strong enough to win a war are not always strong enough to hold onto peace. Around the Table sat men, the King included, who had known nothing but conflict, struggle and war and old ways die hard. Arguments arose between former brothers-in-arms, conflicts became feuds, jealousy became hatred. Finally, a duel to the death between two knights over some matter of honor tore the court's unity asunder and the peace was lost.

"It was then that I declared my quest. I swore to find the Last Cup of our Lord and Saviour and return with it to my King, so that he may drink from it, first of all, and thereby cleanse his soul. Then he could pass it on to his knights so that each could be of pure heart. For I had seen that only then could peace prevail.

"I have been searching all these long years since," Gawain concluded.

"Goodness, Gawain, that is some story!" Jescinta exclaimed. "But I feel that is not the half of it. While I understand your torment at your country's ills and your frustration in finding the cure, I do not think I yet fully understand the sadness I see in you and hear in your voice. Go on, tell me more, but do forgive me if I fall asleep, for your voice is like a lullaby and I am ever so tired."

"As you wish, my lady," Gawain assented before continuing. "Some while ago, I rode into a great city far to the east of here. I had heard of this empire's great wealth and I hoped I might find there the great treasure I sought.

"I found the city in a state of shock and despair. The emperor's daughter, Amora, had disappeared. I learned that the princess was the fairest in the empire and especially close to the emperor's heart. The entire army had searched fruitlessly and the emperor was growing demented.

"Naturally, I swore to find the princess. I rode out into the country with my squire Bart and spoke with the people I met there. I listened closely to whispered conversations in taverns and markets, and I gathered that a giant called Oric had long loved the princess. The emperor had scoffed at the giant's offer of marriage, causing his heart to flame all the hotter. Oric was suspected by many of kidnap but, because his size and strength were feared by all, none were eager to find him.

"Following various clues, we headed into the wilderness of the mountains that bordered the empire. We had seen no one for several days when we came to a small cottage in the wood. An old woman answered the door and eyed me suspiciously. She refused us food and drink and slammed her door in my face. This was such uncommonly bad manners, especially in such a wilderness where people are normally so welcoming, that I kept my eye on the cottage. Presently, I saw a raven fly out from the chimney and head for the nearby peaks. Suspecting it was a messenger, I rode at a gallop to keep the bird in view and so left Bart to follow along behind at his own pace. I was eager to know who would receive the news of my arrival.

"I proceeded up a rocky ravine where I had lost sight of the raven, the air growing colder the higher I went. I rode into a high valley, frozen and treeless, with snowy peaks all around. There stood an enormous castle of rough stone, towering like one of the neighbouring mountains. It was like any pile of stones you might see in the mountains, larger ones gathered at the bottom and smaller ones at the top, only it was far bigger than anything nature could contrive. As I studied the tower of rock, I realized it was circular, wide at the base and narrowing at the top in a perfect conical shape. There were gaps in the stone here and there, making windows and doorways, and a broad walkway spiralled around the peak to the top where a little cloud gathered. Icicles hung everywhere, glistening in the weak sun against the dark rock of the castle. There was no movement or sound—it was as quiet and still as any mountain.

"I rode up to the enormous wooden door at the tower's base and pounded on it with the handle of my sword. A little flap opened and a face appeared, that of the old woman I had met in the wood. She winced when she saw me and then she snarled, 'Who goes there!' I explained who I was and that I had come for the princess Amora. She glared at me with both hatred and fear and then she slammed shut the flap. I backed away from the door and waited for what seemed a long while.

"Presently, the huge door swung slowly open, as if by its own accord, and I rode warily into the great entrance hall of the giant's castle, the slow clatter of Equis' hooves echoing in the empty chamber. The hall was poorly lit by torches here and there and when the door creaked shut behind me, my eyes had to adjust to the faint light. A long corridor stretched ahead from across the room, a single torch burning in the distance. On either side, rough stairways swept up and around and I watched them both in turns for my enemy's advance.

"But when I looked back to the corridor across from me, there he stood, his huge bulk filling the entrance. The giant Oric glared at me with dark bloodshot eyes. His mouth, half covered by a thick and matted beard, smiled cruelly with blackened, grinding teeth. His nostrils flared, snorting out my scent. He was thrice the height of a tall man and as broad as an oak with great slabs of muscles straining. He wore only a short skirt of bear furs and in one gnarled hand he dragged a club fashioned from ironwood. He walked heavily out into the centre of the hall and sniffed the air like one might do to a bowl of stew, grinning at me.

"I could see no reason for talk and I prepared for battle with a prayer for strength. Equis tensed beneath me, ready, and he shot off in a charge when I raised my sword. As I sped toward Oric, he raised his club and swung it for my head when I approached. I ducked and landed my sword feebly into his ribs as I passed. The wound seemed not to pain him, rather it increased his fierceness and when I next charged, he bellowed his rage and slammed his club to the floor as I passed.

"Again and again I rode Equis at the giant, trying to sink home my sword while evading the wicked club. Finally, Oric aimed his blow not at me but my mount, striking Equis squarely on the side of the head and sending us both tumbling. I scrambled to my feet in time to retrieve my sword and avoid the next swing of the club. I was relieved to see Equis stumble to his feet, dazed but unhurt.

"Fighting the giant on foot was a different matter. Even with my long sword, I could barely reach his waist and all I could do was stab and swing at his huge, hairy legs. Despite my armour, I was quicker than he, but still his club sometimes found its mark, paining me terribly, bashing my ribs, smashing my shoulders and knocking my helmet flying. Tasting my own blood in my mouth, I was forced to retreat up one of stairways.

"He followed me up closely and I found myself outside, backing up the walkway that spiralled around the castle walls. It had grown dark and a freezing rain was falling, making the footing slippery and treacherous. On and on we fought, higher and higher up the evil castle. I was forced to block Oric's terrible club with my sword and duck and dive, but more and more I failed and he was able to rattle my bones with his blows. I grew battered and tired so that as we approached the top, I could barely lift my weapon. Thunder began to roll around the surrounding mountains and lightning would now and then flash, showing me the giant's evil face.

"Coming finally to the top of the castle, I stepped up onto the final rampart from which I had no further retreat. I stood there exhausted and gasping and he came after me. I raised my sword one last time and he swung his club, knocking me down and sending my sword clattering over the edge. I lay there helplessly as he stood above me and I could but pray as he raised his club over his head to finish me off.

"Just then there was a terrible crack that shook the castle and a blinding flash of light that briefly lit the sky and the mountains all around. I remember seeing the giant's face contort in pain. I managed to roll away as he fell thudding down next to me. I saw the smouldering black hole in Oric's back where the fatal lightning had struck him before I fainted.

"I awoke to see the worried face of Bartalemew and the angelic face of Princess Amora. I was aware first of all of a warm dry bed and then of pain I cannot describe. Princess Amora nursed me for many days, bathing my wounds, holding my head as she offered me drink and food, changing my bedding when I fouled it and embracing me tenderly when the pain became too much to bear alone. When I was able to mount Equis, we rode out with Amora sat where you are now to support me in my weakness.

"News of our approach spread before us and as we entered the emperor's city, huge, joyful crowds lined the way, shouting rapturously. We entered the palace and were ushered into the throne room, where all the empire's dignitaries were gathered in welcome. The emperor sat upon his throne waiting, tears of joy and gratitude brimming in his eyes. He came forward and embraced his daughter and then, before the gathering, he embraced me like a son. Then in words solemn and measured, he offered me the hand in marriage of his beloved daughter Amora and, thereby, the succession to his throne.

"I looked to the fair maiden who stood there hopefully and need I tell you of the love that had grown between us during the long days of my recovery and journey from the wilderness?

"The gathering waited for my reply and none more so than my true love and at that moment I remembered my quest, the troubled kingdom I had sworn to save and the holy relic I had sworn to find. I could but mutter my pledge to return. I turned and walked slowly away from my love and her father's throne, my heart breaking with each step. And, well, here I am."

Jescinta was overwhelmed by the knight's story.

"Poor Gawain," was all she could say, as she lay her head against his back, wrapping her arms around him in a comforting hug. Finally, she asked, "Gawain, will you know this treasure you seek so desperately when you find it, this marvellous cup of your lord and saviour?"

"Aye, my lady, for sure. It is a small wooden bowl, the sort a poor carpenter once drank from long ago," he answered softly.

Chapter 11

Bartalemew's Song

From behind her, Jescinta heard a soft twanging note. She looked around and saw Bartalemew watching her and holding a strange wooden musical instrument. It had a round base and a long neck with strings stretched along it. With one hand he fiddled with little knobs at the end as he tested the strings with the other, his head tilted listening.

"Bartalemew, I had nearly forgotten you," she said. "I now know a good deal about Gawain, but I know nothing about you. Please, tell me something about yourself."

The boy sat upright, his body stiffening and his face turning crimson. The muscles of his neck and jaw strained and his eyes bulged. His mouth opened and he appeared locked in a desperate struggle.

"I-I-I-I-I," he stammered, taking a big gulp of air. "Www—waa-uhhhh-ss b-b-bo-bo-bor-bor-bornnn...a...a... llll-lol-llolnn-..., opoo!, a ll-llo-, ahgh!"

Jescinta watched his face contort into a twitching grimace, spittle flying everywhere and his head shaking uncontrollably. Frustration, anger and fear flashed in his eyes as he struggled to speak.

"Steady on, dear boy," Gawain called out. "The lady asked a simple question, there is no need to get into a state of apoplexy. Forgive him, mistress Jescinta, the boy cannot help it if he splutters and sprays spittle over all who are within reach. He has a terrible affliction of speech that strikes him all but dumb from time to time. Tragically, it is especially bad at times such as this, when he is most keen to make a good impression. Just when he wants to be at his most charming and eloquent, instead of a gay greeting or a warm welcome, the listener is delivered a torrent of stutters and profanities that offends even the most courteous of people. But when this boy opens his mouth to sing, another story is told. You are forgiven for disbelieving me when I say that you will have never heard a sweeter sound. The songbirds go quiet when squire Bart strikes up a tune. Bartalemew, give us a song."

The boy gave a broad smile, strummed a few notes, and opened his golden throat.

Oh look up now
and gather around,
all ye people fair and worthy.
Clo-ose your eyes
and follow the sound
of the voice of Bartalemew.

Listen to him
sing the song
that will change your dreams forever.
Ta-ap your toes
and sing along
to the song of Bartalemew!

The boy's voice rang out, trailing and trilling as it called his name at the end of the opening verses. Jescinta was startled by the clarity and pitch of the boy's voice. High notes and low were flung out with careless strength, rising into the forest canopy in a fluid, sparkling eddy of sound. Each word of the song was sung with perfect pronunciation and rhythm and color, none of the stuttering and spitting that marred his spoken introduction. The boy even looked different, sitting up and relaxed, moving easily with the motion of his ox, his head raised and face smooth, none of the bent over, screwed up, tense look he gave when he had tried to talk to her earlier. Jescinta fell into a silent listening, waiting expectantly for each new enchanting note of the song. She was aware that she was not alone in her quiet absorption. The whole forest seemed to try to still itself in order to better hear the boy's song. Jescinta saw that what Gawain had said was true, even the songbird pauses to listen when the squire Bart begins to sing.

You will hear a tale
you will want to retell
around fires and tables and bars.
A tale so sweet
that only the ring of the bell
can truly proclaim its full glory!

Hear how the young shepherd,
who would sing to his flock,
will leave the green hills forever.
He will sorely be missed
with every tick of the clock
by the loved ones he left far behind.

Your heart will ache
as much as the boy's
who left so much love far behind.

But leave he must
for far greater joys
beyond yonder hills dost lie.

Jescinta, startled by the opening verses' clear, cheerful call for attention, was now affected by the more solemn tone and timber of these last lines. She thought how far she had come and what she might have left behind.

Hear how the boy,
out searching for strays,
came upon the fallen knight Sir Gawain.
His armour shone brightly
like it held the Sun's rays,
but he was cold and lifeless and still.

Know that the young shepherd
he did kneel to embrace
the head of the stricken Sir Gawain.
Feel what the boy felt
as he gazed upon the face
that was beauty and grace intertwined.

Breathe as the boy does
as he sings out his love
right in the mouth of the dying knight.
Pray as the boy does
as he waits for the dove
to return to the heart of the fallen.

Rejoice as the boy does
when the knight opens his eyes
to smile his grateful return.
Gaze as the boy does
into pools of blue skies
that sparkle with courage and love.

"I swear," the boy sings
from way deep in his heart.
"That I will forever serve this fine man.
I will go where he leads
and study his art,
so that I might be so fine as he."

The boy nursed the broken man
in his rough shepherd's hut,
bringing fresh milk and wild mountain honey.

He mended the bones
and sewed up the cuts,
singing a lullaby all the while.

So the knight did grow strong
and get up on his feet,
saying he must be away with the dawn.
He thanked the young shepherd,
so glad he was to meet
a young man of such fine qualities.

"Where do you go?
For there I will go too
and together we'll ride with the dawn."
"I search for a treasure
I will share with you
if you will sing of our Quest."

He swore that he would
and together they rode
leaving the green hills behind with the dawn.
Thus on that glad day
began this heart warming ode
of the knight's squire, Bar-ta-a-a-le-mew!

These last verses were sung in a slow crescendo, the notes rising to the high canopy of the forest and reverberating through the columns of tree trunks like the voice of a choir filling a cathedral. Then the song picked up tempo and rhythm.

So gather 'round ye good worthies,
let all the tales be told
of the bravest of knights, Sir Gawain.
He quests on and on
for a treasure greater than gold,
leaving legends and love where he goes.

His victories they are legion,
he has lost more than a few,
as he travels the world far and wide.
And all over they sing
these songs I give to you,
so all herald the knight and his Quest!

Jescinta still held Gawain around the waist to steady herself behind him. When the boy began these last two verses, she felt the knight straighten in his saddle. He was taunt with listening, his head high and alert to hear what praise the child would sing. He breathed deeply with expectation, his heart filling with pride and humility in turns with each beat. As the boy sang, the knight felt his back grow stronger, his purpose clearer, his devotion deeper.

Hear tell of his conquests
in the name of his Lord,
whose love turns his arm into steel.
Know of the ogres and witches
and worms that have roared
when Gawain's sword their sorry fate did seal.

Feel the joy and the pain
felt by folk the world wide
where once rode a saviour named Gawain.
Grow so sad once again
as away he doth ride
on his lonely search for the Prize.

See who rides there all right,
close behind the good knight,
only the young squire Bartalemew.
Hear the songs that are sung
by the folk of his might,
taught by the young squire Bartalemew.

Go to the mountains
and all around the seas
as the squire trails behind his knight.
Follow this song now
and see what I sees,
as clear as ray of dawn light.

Learn who tricked the witch
when to the giant Gawain fell-
none other than the squire Bartalemew.
Remember who sang the songs
that were the first to foretell
of the love between knight and princess.

See Equis bravely rise
up on his hind feet
so the knight's sword the higher could reach.
Hear of its death screams
as its heart fails to beat
when the sword slices the loathsome Leech.

*Learn as the boy does
the people's songs and their speech,
so he can teach them to sing of this deed.
Now wherever you goes,
a mother her child she do teach
the songs of Sir Gawain and Bartalemew.*

*Hear how the knight fares
in his search far and wide
for the cup of his Lord and Saviour.
Know that the knight seeks
that from which evil will hide,
for his King's heart Sir Gawain would cleanse.*

*Hear how the knight rides
in his effort to find
the end of his great journey.
For Gawain he does seek
the source of all peace of mind
and rest will he not 'till its his.*

The boy's voice now rang out in peels of thrilling trills and swinging rings, the notes piercing the hushed forest as if he was calling a crowd on market day. His face, flushed and smiling, suggested he held a surprise in store, a verse he composed as he sang.

*And if listen you do,
you will hear a new song
sung by the young squire Barthalemew.
You will hear of a girl,
so fair and so strong,
who rides to save a city from its fate.*

*What songs will I sing
when I've rode in the light
of the young wizardess Jescinta?
Stay by a while
and in notes clear and bright,
I will sing of her beauty and glory!*

Jescinta's face flushed at these last verses. She raised her hand to her mouth to stifle her nervous giggles. What would this cheeky boy sing about her? She would not know, for the knight raised his hand in a call for silence and the boy fell still.

"Bartalemew, I tremble to say this when you are in full song, like the messenger quivers before the tyrant," the knight said. "But tell you I must that we will soon enter the hearing of the Horsacks. Should one note of your song reach their dirty ears, I have no doubt they shall fall over each other to hasten in a horde to the source of the sweet sound. We're not ready for that.

"My lady Jescinta, to you I beg greater leave," Gawain pleaded in apology. "Just as he is about to proclaim his praise of your beauty and grace, I stop the boy's song. For this sin, I shall bear a burden. But I know him. He would go on for some time. Then he would begin to sing of my adventures and the Quest and in an even greater volume, he would tell of his own part in these battles. All of this would take the better part of the day, and once he gets going there is no stopping him. Every time I hear the song, verily every time the boy sings it, it changes in ways wonderful and new. So rightly, I say, that the praise of the singer should outweigh that of the knight and his Quest and even of the fair wizardess. I have seen the thrush fall from its perch as if dead, stricken by the swoon of love it felt for the singer of the Song of Bartalemew."

Jescinta didn't know what to say. She held out her hand and the boy hurried his ox forward so he could take it. He smiled up at her, his face asking 'Did you like my song? Did you hear what I did? Can you guess what comes next?' If Bartalemew had a tail, he would have wagged it.

"That was...!" the girl exclaimed, struggling to find the words. But she gave up, deciding to just say the obvious. "Simply beautiful!"

The boy sighed, satisfied, and they rode hand in hand in silence.

"Wherever we have travelled," Gawain said, "Barthalemew has sung of our Quest and all who have listened have thrilled to his song. Kings, high priests, and emperors have pleaded with him to stay in their castles and temples, promising untold glory and riches. But he has declined. He has chosen to accompany me and follow my treacherous Quest. For this, his friendship and devotion to my cause, I am eternally grateful."

Jescinta felt the great love between the man and the boy, a love strong enough to see them through all of their trials, maybe strong enough to lead to the conclusion of their Quest, maybe strong enough to help in her effort to save Allsworthy.

Chapter 12

Allsworthy, at Last

Late afternoon found the small party of travelers winding down through wooded hills to the valley of Allsworthy. Coming to a small slow stream, they paused to let the mounts have a much deserved drink when Jescinta was startled by a welcome in a friendly voice.

"Greetings, mistress. I see you have arrived just as you promised. It is a pleasure and a relief to see you, I must say," she heard. She looked to where the voice seemed to come from and at first she saw no one. Then she realized that what appeared to be a grey stick stuck in the mud of the stream's shallows was in fact the great heron Blue. She smiled when she recognized him and he seemed to smile back although not a muscle moved in his still, solemn form.

"Blue! What a surprise and a pleasure it is to see you here! How is the hunting?" she asked.

"I fear the hunting gets worse, mistress. Frogs are wily creatures and they can smell danger in the wind. That is why they require a hunter of special skills and patience, such as myself, if I may say so. But these times are trying even my patience, for the presence of this dreadful human army in our valley is seeping everywhere and my prey, sensing their threat, stay safely hidden," he answered in his old formal way. "As for your surprise at meeting me here, mistress Jescinta, it is no accident as I have been waiting for you."

"Of course. I'm sorry, Blue, if I have kept you waiting. I have met some delays along the way, I'm afraid," she answered apologetically.

"As I can imagine, mistress. There is no need to apologize, however, for I think you have arrived in time. The castle still holds," Blue replied and then he stood even stiller and more silent, as if waiting.

Jescinta realized then that she had not yet introduced her two companions to Blue. She looked to Gawain and Bartalemew and she saw them stuck in one of their strange shocked looks she was getting to know so well. She realized then the surprise they must feel at seeing her converse with a heron, as they knew so little about her.

"Oh, Gawain, Bartalemew, I'm sorry. Please, let me introduce you to my friend, Blue," she said, nodding toward the great bird. As the man and boy remained frozen in their open-mouthed surprise and did not speak, Blue thought he had better say something.

"Welcome, sirs, to Allsworthy," he said, lowering his noble head in a graceful bow with a slow sweep of his great neck. Jescinta understood what he said, but Gawain and Barthalemew heard only the muted screechings of a very strange heron. "Friends of our mistress Jescinta are always welcome here in Allsworthy. Would that you had arrived but two or three moons previous, for then you would have found this little shire the most pleasantest on earth and you would have been assured a warm and friendly welcome from the people of Allsworthy. I fear, however, that you have arrived to find this poor place in a state of extreme unease and your visit will not be a pleasant one."

Jescinta said she would explain more later about her talking with Blue, and then she translated the heron's greeting. When they realized that they had been addressed in a gallant speech of welcome by a tall bird, Gawain and Bartalemew returned the greeting, the knight with a slow nod of his head, the boy with a little tug at his forelock.

Blue then went on to humbly suggest that his mistress Jescinta may wish to consider resting here awhile on the grassy bank of this fruitful stream with her most welcome friends. He explained that here they were safely beyond the malevolent reach of the main Horsack camp, which lay directly between them and the Castle Allsworthy. The castle could be reached quickly with a short flight around the invader's camp and Blue then said that he had taken the liberty of arranging for them to make their entry into Allsworthy later that evening. He would explain more of the arrangements later, he explained, and then he asked:

"Frogs, anyone?"

Jescinta did not understand the question and when she translated it to her companions, they were none the wiser.

"Frogs, Blue? What ever do you mean?" Jescinta asked.

"Mistress, forgive me if I cause confusion," Blue apologized. "It's just that we have some little time to rest and gather our energies. I was intending a bit of a late lunch, and I only meant to offer you as guests a share of my humble fare. Frogs, anyone?"

Jescinta, understanding Blue now, replied with a hurried "No, thank you." Gawain and Bartalemew, guessing the general flow of the discussion, gave their firm but polite refusals.

Jescinta and Gawain sat in the shade of a willow to talk while Barthalemew unpacked his ox and led it into the stream. The girl explained the way some animals could sometimes talk with her and how she could somehow talk to them. She also explained about the location of the Horsack camp and Blue's arrangements for them to get into the castle.

"Now, Gawain, I know you have had a lot of surprises today, and I wouldn't want you to overdo it," she continued. "But there is one thing I have to do now that you might find a little surprising. Before I met you, I had two other traveling companions. They will be wondering where I am and, if it's all right with you, I'll call them now."

With that she took out her horn and gave it a loud blast. In not too long a time, Oo-oo-luf landed silently in the willow.

"Uhm, hello, mistress," he finally said, once he'd had a good long look at Gawain, studied Bartalemew and the ox wallowing in the water, the stallion grazing and Blue hunting carefully upstream, and after he'd stretched his neck and fluffed his feathers.

"Oo-oo-luf, how good of you to arrive so quickly," Jescinta said. "Let me introduce my friend the knight Gawain. He has promised to help us with our trouble in Allsworthy."

Gawain, growing accustomed to being introduced to birds when in this girl's company, scrambled clankingly to his feet to bow deeply and creakily from the waist. Oo-oo-luf watched him closely with his two big orange eyes before finally blinking one slowly shut to make his greeting.

Jescinta explained about the nearby Horsack camp, Blue's plan to gain them entry into Allsworthy later that evening and of her wish to know more about the enemy.

"Mistress, wish no more, for if it is within my power. I shall personally see that you know all you need to know of the invaders' camp," Oo-oo-luf replied with all the self-importance he could muster. Then he flew off as silently as he arrived.

No sooner had the owl passed from sight then Jescinta and Gawain began to hear the soft thudding of hooves approaching through the wood. Gawain made to get to his feet once again, expecting the arrival of a Horsack rider, but Jescinta stilled him with her hand upon his arm.

"That will be my other companion," she explained.

They listened as the thudding hooves approached. Urun came through the undergrowth into the little meadow just near the willow and froze in a stance of alertness and readiness. Jescinta got to her feet and walked slowly towards him, talking softly. She held her hand out as she drew near and stroked his muzzle. She whispered in his ear and then motioned for Gawain to come forward. The knight clamoured quietly forward and, when he came near the stag, bowed deeply from the waist. Urun gave the strange man a good look and then lowered his great head with a long sweep of his neck, his antlers scything the air. Gawain smiled and so did Jescinta. No one said a word yet each understood the other. Together, they walked back to the shade of the willow and got comfortable.

Lying in the crooks of the willow's roots and leaning against its trunk, they watched Blue proceed toward them from his hunting grounds in the shallows of the stream and up onto the bank in his purposeful, stately walk. Just as he came within the tree's shaded circle, a pigeon arrived, landing noisily on a branch just above the heron's head.

"Duchess! How expedient of you to arrive in such timely fashion!" Blue exclaimed. "Let me introduce you. Jescinta, Wizardess of Canabria, your colleague, the stag king Urun, and your new companion, Gawain of the Table, please meet Duchess, her ladyship, queen of the royal messenger service and beloved favourite of good King Lufalot of Allsworthy."

The pigeon puffed up her chest feathers and arched her neck to look at the three visitors with her startling green eyes.

"Such a pleasure to meet you, my Lady Jescinta," Duchess cooed. "I have heard such a lot about you from our dear friend Blue and I see with pleasure that you are everything he said you were."

Jescinta returned her greeting and marvelled at the beauty of the royal pigeon. Her huge green eyes shone from her noble purple head and her strong neck set poised upon her plump, white feathered body, flecked with violet. Her slim orange legs supported gracefully her perfect bulk and her long toes curled around the branch.

Blue explained that Duchess was said to be more beloved of the King than the Queen herself and would surely deliver directly to King Lufalot a message from the wizardess Jescinta. The heron suggested that the girl write on a slip of paper that the King should lower the castle's drawbridge when 'the birds arrive.' Jescinta did as he suggested and then secured the note to the little leather pouch on the pigeon's leg. The pigeon blinked meaningfully at the newcomers and then fluttered off noisily through the leaves of the willow before she sped off toward Castle Allsworthy.

"We should go soon," Blue said.

While Gawain and Bartalemew made last minute preparations with Equis and the ox, Jescinta spoke with her mount.

"Urun, you know you don't have to go with us," she said. "I know how nervous you get around humans and I'm very grateful that you have been able to befriend Gawain. But the Castle Allsworthy will be a different matter. It is crowded with humans, frightened and maybe hungry humans. I'm sure no harm would come to you as my companion, but I fear you would feel uncomfortable in the presence of so many people."

"I'm sure I will, mistress, and thank you for thinking of me thus," Urun replied. "I said I would take you to Allsworthy and so I shall. True, when I made my promise I had not thought about entering a castle full of humans, but I will just have to contain the fear I know I shall feel and be thankful that I can fulfill my promise."

Jescinta gave him a little hug before swinging up onto his thick shoulders. She rode in front with Bartalemew behind and Gawain bringing up the rear. Blue led the way, flying on a little ahead and waiting for the riders to catch up. They had to look carefully to see him perched in trees or stood upon a log, as his tall stillness never failed to fool them. Once they had spotted him, he would fly on ahead again, staying low to glide beneath the spread limbs of the forest.

Finally blue waited until they caught up with him and they saw that their journey was nearly completed . Through the leaves, they could see that the forest stopped abruptly to give way to the open pasture land that stretched around the Castle Allsworthy. The fortress stood brooding sullenly beneath a clump of dark rain cloud that towered above it in a tall cylinder of swirling vapors. The thick walls of cut stone were darkened by the steady rain that ran dripping off them and into the wide moat, the surface of which dappled with each drop of the downpour. A bright rainbow arched in the sunlight beyond the castle's dark cloud, where a spark of light occasionally flashed and a low rumble would follow. The great drawbridge faced them, closed up to bar the way, its oak beams blackened with rain.

Just opposite the drawbridge and along the road from the castle, Jescinta and her companions could see a sentry of six Horsack warriors. They waited near the forest edge, huddled around a small cooking fire. Their horses stood tethered nearby, ready to ride off to the main camp to sound a warning at a moment's notice. Jescinta was struck by the soaking silence of the brooding castle, the empty, ungrazed pasture, the Horsack guards waiting in the evening sunlight and the quiet forest where not a bird twittered. Urun moved forward a little to get a better look, his hooves rustling in the dry leaves.

"As you can see," Blue finally said to Jescinta. "There is a difficulty with getting into the castle. The moment the drawbridge begins to creak open, one of the Horsack sentries will ride off to alert the main camp. The remaining five will harry your race to the bridge and there will be but a short time before the main host of the Horsack cavalry is racing forward to pour into the castle. I have taken the liberty of arranging a small diversion. You will have to wait here quietly for a while, but when you see the birds, that will be your signal to move. Now, if I may be excused, I will see to some last minute preparations."

With that, the heron flew quietly off through the trees. A few moments later they saw him flying just above the treetops, circling behind the castle and then disappearing from view behind the cloud without so much as a glance from the Horsack sentries.

Just then, Oo-oo-luf arrived, landing unnoticed on a branch behind Jescinta who was watching closely for Blue's signal, whatever that was going to be.

"So here you are," he hooted softly, causing the girl to whirl around on Urun's back. "I have been searching for you, but fortunately you were easy to find. Are you in hiding from those six chaps over there?" he asked, indicating with a little swivel of his head the Horsack sentries. "If so, I hope they don't find you as easy to find as I do. That would be most unwelcome, as they look as if they mean business."

"Hello, Oo-oo-luf, I knew you would find us. I think we are safe here," she whispered. She then explained their wait for Blue's signal, whatever that was going to be, and asked, "Did you find the Horsack camp? What do you have to tell?"

"Did I find them, mistress? Hmmmff. What a question. A blind crow could have found the foul place, I assure you. It can be smelled, believe me, from some distance. Can't you imagine the stench of a thousand warriors stuck for weeks in a damp woodland? The reek of their unwashed bodies and clothes, the suffocation of their fires, the pong of their kitchens, slaughter houses and latrines. and their infernal horses, two for every man, constantly peeing and pooing. Surely even you could have found the Horsack camp, with all respect, mistress. Even if you were bereft of the sense of smell, you could surely hear their loud voices shouting, swearing and singing, their clanging and scraping as they make and sharpen their weapons, and the constant nagging, neighing and ninnying of their wretched horses. Oh yes, mistress, I found the Horsack camp.

"And as for what I have to tell, there is this: When I arrived minutes after leaving you, I found the Horsacks gathered in some kind of meeting. The largest number stood or sat in the camp's central compound, facing their leader who sprawled upon cushions and carpets spread out in the shade of an elm. To either side of this general sat lesser leaders, his captains, I suppose, and to his right and just behind him sat bolt upright a large black dog. This dog was strange, even for a pet. He did not move throughout the meeting except to turn his head a little to face whoever happened to be speaking and I felt he was paying very close attention to everything that was said.

"I was perched on some large wooden contraption, one of several of different sorts of machines they had hewn from the trees. I watched safely unnoticed as one after another the warriors stepped forward to the space in front of the reclining general and spoke their mind. The general watched impassively

as each speaker out did the one before in drama and length of speech. There
was much beating of breasts and pointing toward the south. Again and again
they rubbed their foreheads with the palm of one hand, clutched an amulet
they all wore around their neck with the other and muttered some kind of
oath. There was much complaining. They would point to the trees, scowl and
screech like a bird and then look up to the hill tops, growl and spit high into
the air.

"When it seemed that the men had their say, the general sat as
motionless and unmoved as he had done throughout the performance. Then I
saw the dog lean forward, putting his muzzle close to the man's ear as if sniffing
or licking in the way such pet creatures do. Now the general moved, getting
swiftly to his feet and barking out his decision in a few sharp words. Then he
turned and walked firmly towards a large tent. I noticed the dog stayed put,
watching the gathering break up. The warriors walked away to their weapons
and their horses, mumbling and grumbling.

"A group of men came towards the contraption I was perched upon and
one of them noticed me. He shouted and pointed and instantly the whole camp
turned their shocked faces toward me. In unison they rubbed their foreheads,
clutched their amulets, muttered their oaths and raced for their weapons. I flew
for the treetops, dodging arrows until I was out of sight. I circled and came
down unnoticed behind the big tent. I could hear the clamor and shouting of
the camp as the warriors watched the treetops for me, letting their arrows loose
at the slightest movement.

"I poked my head under the tent and saw the general sat upon a hard
pallet. He looked tired and drawn, not at all like one preparing for battle. He
opened a small wooden chest and took from it several objects: a long lock of
black hair, a miniature bow and arrow and the small form of a girl made from
straw. Then the man did this curious thing that humans do, when water streams
from their eyes, their shoulders shake uncontrollably and they wail and blubber
and wring their hands. Most curious. Just then, the dog walked in. He stood
in front of the poor man and shook his head as if in disgust. Then he sprawled
down upon a pile of firs and proceeded to lick himself in the shameless manner
these dog creatures tend to do."

"Well thank you very much, Oo-oo-luf. That's very helpful. Later,
I'll tell your news to Gawain, who I'm sure will understand it better than I,"
Jescinta whispered once the owl had finished his report. Then she turned to
watch the sky for Blue's signal, gradually becoming as still and uneasy as the
strange silence that filled the evening air.

Chapter 13

Allsworthy Under Siege

It began as a faint squeak coming from the forest beyond the castle and its cloud, a sound so small that Jescinta would never have noticed it if she had not been listening carefully to the queer silence. The squeak became a quiet shrill whistle and then it grew into a dull shriek in the distance. The shriek became a screech and then a scream as the sound grew quickly louder and apparently closer. In amongst the scream could be heard twitters, hoots, caws and quacks.

Jescinta saw that the Horsack sentries had noticed the growing cacophony, as they stood and stared tensely at the treetops beyond the castle. She felt Urun stiffen beneath her, alarmed at the noise. Gawain and Bartalemew gripped the reins of their mounts and all eyes strained toward the rushing sound. But there was nothing to see there, only the increasing din to hear, until a dark line suddenly burst through the cloud just above the castle walls. The line flew down the wall and became a wave that swelled across the open land, skimming the ground. The wave became a sharp wedge of noise, headed directly for the Horsacks.

It took Jescinta a moment to remember Blue's instructions about the signal, but when she realized this was it, she spurred Urun on and they burst from the forest to make the run for the castle. Glancing over her shoulder, she saw Barthalemew had followed her and Gawain reined in his Equis in order to trail along behind the slower ox.

Bounding toward the castle, Jescinta saw firstly that the great drawbridge had begun to open and secondly that one of the Horsacks had turned to run toward his horse, just as Blue had predicted. Thirdly, she saw the wedge of noise had become a speeding spear of birds, with the great heron Blue at its tip. Behind him flew all the flying, feathered creatures of Allsworthy—every crow, songbird and dove that lived in its trees; every duck, coot and bittern that came from its waters; every quail, pheasant and partridge that pecked in its field; every falcon, hawk and eagle that hunted its woodlands. The screeching, singing, whirring spear shot toward the Horsacks and was upon them before they knew what it was. The spear became a cloud as it piled into the enemy, a cloud of flapping and pecking and screaming that enveloped the terrified men.

Drawing near to the lowering bridge, Jescinta saw the Horsacks beginning to fight back, flailing at the air with their short swords and occasionally sending a puff of feathers flying. The would-be messenger had gained his mount and began to speed toward the main camp. Looking over her shoulder, Jescinta saw that Barthalemew had fallen well behind on his slower ox, with Equis straining at his bit as Gawain followed him protectively. When Urun clamored onto the lowered bridge, she saw that one of the remaining Horsacks had managed to mount his horse and come racing to intercept her companions.

She waited on the bridge and watched as Gawain directed Equis away from the castle and toward the oncoming Horsack rider. They met at full gallop, their swords clashing frightfully. The two warriors circled each other, their weapons flashing, their horses prancing and colliding excitedly.

Barthalemew reached the bridge and he and the girl watched as the cloud of birds began to disperse, their mission completed, allowing the remaining Horsacks to hurry toward their horses. Frightened voices from within the castle called to them and they moved slowly, reluctantly across the rain-soaked bridge into the safety of the stone walls. Looking over their shoulders, they saw the other Horsacks coming quickly toward their friend.

Gawain saw them, too, and knew he had no time to lose. Equis was much bigger than the Horsacks' ponies and Gawain used his weight to guide their adversary toward the moat. The grey charger lowered his head and lunged forward, butting the pony and rider over the edge and into the water. The bridge began to creak slowly up, and Gawain saw the four enemy horsemen would beat it and manage to race into the castle. He also saw that emerging from the forest and speeding along the road to the castle was the rest of the Horsack cavalry. If the four riders gained entry into the castle, they could force the drawbridge down and allow the enemy army to come pouring into the castle.

The knight turned his horse once again away from the castle and charged toward the four advancing Horsacks, who rode side by side in a fearsome line. Coming near, he veered across their path and with a mighty swing of his long sword, knocked two to the ground and caused the others' horses to stop and rear to avoid the blade. Then Equis spun around and surged toward the castle, his hooves churning the ground. Drawing close, Equis broke from his gallop and fell into a bounding canter. He gathered himself as he approached the moat's edge, Gawain gave a shout of encouragement, and he sprung upward toward the rising bridge, now well above his head. They floated through the air and above the water, Equis' front hooves just catching the edge of the rising bridge. Horse and rider hung there a moment suspended in silence, Gawain gave another call for strength and the Horsack cavalry thundered forward and arrows zinged through the air. With one last mighty effort of his powerful shoulders, Equis raised his great weight and that of his master, found the edge of the bridge with his back foot and heaved himself up, sliding down the tilted bridge into the castle courtyard.

Gawain gave a triumphant war-cry, waved his sword in the air and turned the excited Equis in little circles. Then he stopped, realizing that he rejoiced in his victory alone. The wizardess and his squire looked relieved to see him alive, but the rest—the soldiers and ordinary people of Allsworthy crowded into the courtyard—only stared blankly, silently at him, their faces lined with fear and hopelessness and incapable of joy and triumph. Beyond the closing drawbridge could be heard the menacing howls of the Horsack cavalry, causing the crowd within the castle to shudder and tremble.

Jescinta and Barthalemew rode over to the knight and the girl leaned across to give him a hug to show how glad she was that he had made it safely into the castle. The boy could only look intently, silently at the man who had just risked his life for him and one had to guess the gratitude, admiration and love he felt. Gawain guessed the boy's feelings all right and he showed it with a warm, modest smile that caused Bart's eyes to moisten and his face to flush.

A man stepped forward and announced himself as Marsad, Man-at-Arms to King Lufalot of Allsworthy. He was a tall, powerfully-built, capable-looking general, but middle-aged, soft around the waist, and possessed of the drawn, worried look of a man who knew his fate and didn't like it, an expression Jescinta saw on all the rain-drenched faces that crowded around. Marsad explained that the King would receive them later that evening in the throne room and he offered to show them to their quarters where they could rest until then. The three companions dismounted and Barthalemew led the excited charger, the tired ox and the anxious stag across the muddy courtyard to the stables, singing softly in Urun's ear to soothe his fears.

Gawain faced Marsad, introduced himself in his particular, formal way, pledged allegiance in a firm, loud voice with a clang of his mailed fist against his armoured chest and bowed deeply at the waist. Marsad returned his greeting but with nothing like his vigour. Then he turned to Jescinta.

"Welcome, mistress," he said, bowing half heartedly. "It is a great pleasure to meet you at last, though we would wish for better circumstances."

Jescinta heard a great deal in this short speech: his tiredness at withstanding a long siege by powerful invaders, his hopelessness in preventing a dreadful outcome, his shame in not being able to fulfil his duty as protector of the realm, his fear for his life and the people of Allsworthy and his extreme disappointment at meeting the new wizardess of the district, a mere girl clearly incapable of overpowering the Horsack hordes.

The girl and the knight then followed Marsad through the crowded courtyard and into the castle. He led them to a room where he said they could wait until the king was ready to greet them. He indicated a table where there was prepared a small loaf of bread, a chunk of dry cheese and a jug of water. Marsad apologized for the meager fare, but it was all that could be offered. Before he left, Gawain asked that they meet later so that Marsad could show him the castle's fortifications and they could inspect his troops.

Jescinta and Gawain meted out the bread and cheese, setting aside some for Bart, while the girl told the knight what the owl had reported earlier. Gawain listened in silence, eating quickly, and when he had finished his last mouthful and the girl had finished speaking, he drained his cup in one go, stood, bowed, begged his leave and strode purposely out of the door.

Jescinta, who had been talking so much that she hadn't yet touched her food, began to pick at the bread and cheese. She looked around the room and saw a doorway covered by a heavy curtain. Following her curiosity, she walked across and peaked behind. There she found a little room and in the centre of it a large metal tub of steaming, scented, bubbly water. Just what she needed after a long, tiring journey—a warm bath to soak away the aches and strain and fatigue. Stripping off, she wondered who in this beleaguered city had found the strength in the midst of their despair to be so thoughtful? Settling into the tub, she hoped to thank whoever it was by somehow relieving them of their worries and hopelessness.

While the hot, fragrant bath soaked away the aches and grime of travel, she pondered on the difficult situation that faced her. She thought about Oo-co-luf's report of the strange goings-on in the Horsack camp and then she suddenly remembered her meeting with Goddell in her home in the great oak. It seemed like ages ago but it had only been a couple of days. She remembered an odd question he had asked but did not explain when she queried him.

"Did Blue mention anything about a wizard?" Goddell had enquired after her account of the heron's message. This memory was quickly followed by another, a reliving of an experience hugely significant in the short life of the young wizardess.

On the night of her initiation at the last Gathering of the Wizards, she had trailed along behind as the wizards left their encampment and proceeded in single file up into the hills to a grassy knoll. Waiting for them was a circle of flat stones, one for each wizard to sit upon and one freshly placed for Jescinta. They sat in silence, staring into the centre beneath the glare of a full moon. After a time, each of the wizards took it in turn to come off their stone and go into the centre to speak, telling of their activities since their last meeting, describing some special magic they had performed, reporting on the happenings in their district, commenting on what it means to be a wizard and performing some trick of illusion to entertain their colleagues. Eventually, there were only three left to take their turns: Jescinta, who would be last as she was the newest to the gathering, Goddell and Krael, a small, wizened old man. He stepped forward into the centre.

Krael spoke in a high, urgent voice of the changing times, how the world of humans was growing more crowded, how people were becoming more concerned with worldly things, uncaring of spirit and magic, and less responsive to the word of the wizard. The wizards must change too, he claimed. They needed to abandon their old ways if they were to retain their influence. They needed leadership, the direction of someone strong and wise to see them through these difficult times. And he, Krael, the oldest and mightiest of the wizards was the one to take the lead. He urged them to accept him as their king—he would show them the way, he alone knew the direction into the future of wizardom. He then sought to demonstrate his pre-eminence by taking different shapes. He became a giant moth, fluttering in the moonlight, then a snake, coiled and ready to strike, a roaring lion and a huge screeching eagle. He transformed into a towering stone of granite, unmoving and brooding, and the stone became a pillar of fire, swirling and causing a heated wind to whirl around the circle and threaten to singe the onlookers. The flames gathered together into the shape of a screaming griffon and then a large, black dog, hackles raised, teeth bared, growling. The beast turned to Jescinta and she felt her blood run cold. Then it rose up on its hind legs and became Krael, the old wizard who would be king. He returned to his stone, waiting to be declared the King of the Wizards.

After a long tense silence, Goddell rose from his stone, wearily and slowly. He moved into the centre and looked upward. All the wizards did likewise, studying the full moon and the flickering stars. Goddell held out his hand as if he was beneath an apple tree and waiting for one of its fruit to fall to him. A star in the heavens suddenly glowed brightly and then began to spiral down, trailing a tail of fire. It shot into his upturned hand and he held it gently, eyeing each of the wizards in turn.

"The stars in the heavens each have their own light," he said. "None look to the others for the right to shine or for the wisdom to do so."

He then tossed the star to Jescinta and returned to his stone. The girl jumped up and caught it with both hands, amazed that this was happening. She walked into the centre with the star cupped in her hands. She passed it back and forth from hand to hand, she balanced it on her nose, put it on top of her head and bounced it up with her forehead several times, then slid it down the sleeve of her gown and wiggled and gyrated until it came out of the other sleeve. She tossed it over her head and caught it behind her back, threw it into the air, twirled, clapped her hands ten times and caught it again. Then she slung the star into the air and caught it in her teeth. She waited a moment before she swallowed it with great difficulty, gulping and grimacing.

Then she pulled her wizardess gown up above her waist and, squatting a little and grunting comically, reached down to catch the star as it passed out of her bottom. With a squeal of delight, she hurled the glowing orb upwards to its rightful place in the heavens and returned to her stone. The wizards leapt to their feet cheering and clapping and laughing, while Krael remained seated and defeated, glaring at the girl. With a child such as this performing magic so stunning and irreverent, the point was made clearly that wizards had no need of a king.

Coming out of her revelry, Jescinta heard the door to the other room open and then the clanging boots of Gawain and the soft steps of Barthalemew. She called out to them and reluctantly got out of her bath to join them to wait for the summons to be presented to King Lufalot.

Chapter 14

The Dance of Life

Sometime later, the three travellers were startled by a loud knock on their door. Barthalemew hurried to open it and Marsad stepped in.

"King Lufalot is ready to receive you." he said. Jescinta and her companions followed the Man-at-Arms and a bodyguard of ten soldiers who marched briskly through seemingly endless corridors while occasional sharp cracks of thunder clapped around the castle walls, causing their escort to all flinch in response. Eventually they approached large double doors and as they drew near, guards presented arms and swung the doors open. Marsad led the way into the spacious throne room.

Jescinta saw that the room was crowded with the people of Allsworthy, who stared blankly at her as she followed Marsad across the hall with Gawain and Barthalemew close behind her.

"Your Highness" he announced after a feeble bow, "may I present Jescinta, Wizardess of Canabria."

He stepped aside, leaving Jescinta to face King Lufalot. He sat slumped in his throne, his head held in one hand, his crown slightly askew, his eyes downcast. Beside him sat his Queen, tall, erect, and thin in contrast to her husband's short roundness. Her body betrayed her tension, as her hands played nervously with a string of beads in her lap and her eyes stared wide and expectantly at the young wizardess. She managed a thin smile for the girl and Jescinta, now knowing who to thank for the comforting bath, nodded to show her appreciation.

"Greetings, your Highness" Jescinta said with a deep curtsy as she studied the broken man before her. He had not yet looked up to acknowledge her presence. She saw that his face, whose creases and wrinkles showed that it was more accustomed to laughter and wise warmth, was flaccid and grey with dark circles of worry under the eyes. She felt shock and alarm at the realization that the King was so severely stricken with the helpless, hopeless malady that she had seen in the other occupants of the Castle. "And greetings to the good people of Allsworthy", she declared in a loud voice, looking around the room at the nobles, commoners and soldiers gathered there, each and every one watching her in subdued silence. A rumble of thunder resounded from beyond the castle walls. "I regret that, as your wizardess and servant, we meet for the first time under such dire circumstances. I come, I promise you, to help as best I can in these difficult times. Allow me to introduce my companions, the knight Sir Gawain and his squire, Bartalemew."

Bart bowed deeply and Gawain stepped purposely, noisily forward to the throne. He went down on one knee, clanged his right arm to his armoured chest and bowed his head before rising to speak.

"My Lord, I am but a stranger in your fair land, but please allow me to pledge allegiance to your cause in driving this invader from your castle gates" he pleaded in a loud, sure voice. King Lufalot finally looked up, stirred by the knight's martial tone, and after studying the man before him, gave a small nod of his head. "Your Highness, I have considered the situation carefully and I have several observations to make. First, the Horsacks will end their long siege of your city tomorrow with an all-out assault upon your castle." A cry of alarm went out from the assemblage, women wailed and men shouted. The air boomed and a blinding light pierced through the high windows of the throne room. Gawain raised his arms for silence before continuing. "Second, your castle walls will not withstand the war machines the Horsacks have prepared, the catapults and battering rams they have built while they have waited for you to grow tired and weak." Another, louder outcry erupted and it took a time before Gawain could continue. "Third, the Horsacks have no stomach for a fight. They have long been at war, marauding from city to city, far from their home and families, their warriors yearning to return to their open pastures and their herds, hating the deep forests of Allsworthy. Fourth, your army is strong and well armed with a cavalry as fleet as any. I conclude that our only hope is to strike at once, do not wait and hide and hope against reason, but ride out at first light" he called, raising a fist to the sky, "and drive the enemy from your land!"

Silence in the throne room and a rumble of thunder beyond the walls greeted the knight's call to arms and he bowed before returning to his place. Jescinta took a step forward to speak.

"Your Highness, I believe black magic has been used to drag you and your kingdom into a state of hopelessness and submission. Don't ask how Gawain and I know these things", she said, glancing up at a window where Oo-oo-luf perched watching. "You wouldn't believe me if I told you. Defeat is an evil illusion—victory is a reality if you will but grasp it!"

Yet another crack of thunder answered the girl, followed by a blinding flash of lightning that briefly illuminated the frightened faces of the crowd. King Lufalot could only lean forward and bury his face in his hands, his shoulders shaking in doubt and despair. Finally, his Queen spoke.

"Surely, my dear girl", she said in a high, quivering voice, her head shaking with tension. "One must fight fire with fire. What magic can you promise us if we agree to do as your friend, the knight Gawain suggests?"

"Evil and fear are not defeated by more of the same" Jescinta replied, taking a deep breath. "But by righteousness and courage."

Jescinta then removed her cloak, handing it to Bartalemew who hurried forward, and then her shoulder bag, after taking out her wizardess hat and placing it firmly upon her head. She uncovered her wand and walked toward the centre of the room, the crowd parting to give her space, murmuring and whispering at the sudden transformation of the ordinary appearing girl into something more beautiful and strange. Her dress and hat were a silver white with celestial shapes in soft shades that shimmered with each step. She held her wand high and the crystal at its end grew brighter as it soaked in the light of the torches that hung on the walls all around to illuminate the throne room. Then the young wizardess spun slowly and as she did so, a gust of wind whirled, extinguishing the torches until the room was dark except for the bright crystal of Jescinta's wand and the shimmer of her dress and pointed hat.

Again the crowd murmured and gasped and when they fell quiet, the girl who held their attention began to slowly twirl, moving in small graceful circles. The hem of her wonderful dress billowed as she spun with one arm holding the wand high, the other held out for balance, her head slightly tilted.

The people of Allsworthy watched their wizardess in silence, amazed as much by the strangeness of her behaviour as by the grace of her movements as she spun and circled. She danced in perfect balance to the rhythm of a music she alone could hear. Her eyes were half-opened but unseeing, and she seemed to smile at some inner pleasure they could not guess. When lightning flashed, as it did from time to time, the crystal at the end of her wand would grow a little brighter, lightening the room.

The crowd again broke out into gasps and cries of wonder and surprise as chunks of varied colored light - that's all it can be called - began to emerge from the girl's dress and spread and swirl around the room, some spinning around the ceiling, others close to the floor or passing just beneath their noses, lights like those that can be seen only in the skies of the far North, but here they were in the throne room of the Castle Allsworthy, rotating in rhythm with the girl who was their wizardess.

Gradually the crowd grew quiet again, absorbed by the amazing sights of the slowly spinning girl and the swirling coloured lights. An absolute silence filled the room and soon the people of Allsworthy began to grasp the significance of this silence. No pitter-patter of rain, no crack, rumble and roar of thunder! Again the crowd broke into whispers and gasps as this realization hit them, this liberation from the drone of precipitation and the menace of explosion!

Eventually they grew quiet again while the girl continued to twirl and revolve and the chunks of light swirled with her. The people fell into silent absorption with the beauty of it all, the graceful movement of the girl and the lights to a music beyond their reckoning.

A child in the crowd, a girl who was more of a child than the wizardess, was the first to hear it. She had been straining to hear the music to which Jescinta danced and it was as if the beauty of what she saw as she watched and listened had suddenly unplugged her ears. All at once the girl became aware of the wizardess's music and she realized it had been there all along but unnoticed and unheard, like the sound of her own breathing or the beating of her heart. What the girl suddenly heard and the wizardess danced to was the gentle twinkling of the stars, the shooting zip as they fell, the low throb of the Sun, the high tenor of Venus and deep baritone of Mars, the mournful moan of the Moon, the intricate ring of Saturn and the majestic cool of Jupiter, the surprising roar of the comets, the sprinkle of meteors, and behind it all the steady rhythm of the planet, each blending and supporting the other in a song of perfect harmony.

The girl moved out into the centre with Jescinta and began to twirl as she did, one hand held aloft, the other to the side, her head slightly tilted, listening and now hearing, revolving around the wizardess. Barthalemew followed her out into the open space, then the Queen, Gawain, King Lufalot, Marsad, and one by one all the others until they all danced with the swirling colors of light, moving together in a slowly whirling, twirling, smiling mass as one, their mind empty and free of fear and doubt, free to dance to the music of the spheres. Even Oo-oo-luf, usually so cool and aloof, felt compelled to come off his perch on the high window ledge and fly around in circles above the dancing crowd.

And as they danced, each and every one felt within them a pleasure, a joy, a deep, heartfelt love they had never known before, a sense of purpose and belonging. To the people of Allsworthy, who had known so much fear and despair, this dance with the music of the spheres was like the desert soaking in a sudden shower of rain, or a starving man being offered a spoonful of honey, and their spirits soared to the heavens.

How long they danced, none will ever know. They came slowly to a stop altogether as if they'd practiced it. Each stood alone together marvelling at what they had done before turning to the one closest to share a smile and fall into a warm and vigorous hug. King Lufalot made his way to Jescinta and stood before her smiling, his eyes bright and moist, his face flushed. "Thank you, my dear girl!" he said, giving her a strong embrace. Then he called out in a loud, strong voice that sent shivers of excitement running through his subjects. "People of Allsworthy, hear me! Through the good wizardess Jescinta, we have felt the infinite strength and courage to be found in righteousness unity. I say, to arms! Prepare to ride and drive the enemy from our land!"

Chapter 15

The Battle for Allsworthy

Jescinta stood shivering in the predawn gloom on the bank of the castle moat. When the dance of life had finished, King Lufalot, Marsad and Sir Gawain had hurried off with Bartalemew close behind to prepare for the dawn assault on the invaders. Queen Beatrix had come forward to grasp her hands tightly and stare into her eyes before she also scurried away and then, one by one, each from the crowd came forward to bow and touch her dress before departing while the girl who had first heard her music had stood staring up at her. Jescinta had felt an overwhelming need to be alone with her own thoughts and she had run to the castle ramparts. The bewildered guards had lowered her with ropes and pulleys to this spot beyond the walls.

The rain had stopped, leaving behind a thick, heavy fog. Jescinta's mind was oppressed by a heavy swirl of thoughts and fears she could not stop and grasp. What had she done? The people of Allsworthy were soon going to ride out from the safety of their castle walls to face their enemy in battle because she had urged them to do so. What would happen, who would be victorious, whose lives would be lost through her actions? What orphans and widows would be created, who would be injured and invalid, what pain and terror would ensue because she had danced as she had?

She pulled her cloak tight around her and the hood up over her head to defend against the damp chill. With the moat and castle walls behind her, she peered in vain into a thick, misty darkness where somewhere beyond eye and ear the Horsacks readied themselves for battle. She felt rather than heard a flutter of wings and then a small weight landed on her shoulder.

"Oo-oo-luf," she said, turning her head. "How good of you to join me."

The owl looked deeply into her, his huge yellow eyes trying to weigh her thoughts and feelings before speaking.

"Well, this should be interesting," he finally observed in his cool, knowing way.

"Interesting," she replied, turning back to the fog and the darkness. "That isn't a word I had thought of using. I confess to not knowing what to make of this and I feel a troubling terror at this unknowing."

"At least you are not alone in your unknowing," the owl replied. "You have friends here and behind those walls who do not know and are yet ready to act."

"Friends," Jescinta said quietly, looking off into the dark fog where the enemy gathered. "Oo-oo-luf, I want you to do something for me, something I know will be hard for you. I want you to fly to Wolves' Tor and ask Lupus, the wolf-king to bring his pack to Allsworthy. Will you do this for me?"

"Why mistress? What do you have in mind? How can a bunch of mangy, flea-ridden mongrels be of any use now?" the owl enquired.

"I don't know, Oo-oo-luf," the girl admitted. "Lupus promised his assistance should it be required. I think at times such as this, you can't have too many friends," she said, looking at the little owl with a smile.

"Well, I can think of nothing I'd rather do than fly into the stronghold of a pack of bloodthirsty carnivores to extend an invitation," Oo-oo-luf replied. "Won't be long."

With that, the brave little owl flew silently away, leaving the girl alone with the dark fog and her fears.

She stood still in the silent gloom for what seemed an eternity, not knowing why and not knowing what else she could do. She wondered what Goddell would do in this situation and as soon as she asked herself this question, she heard clearly his deep voice addressing her, speaking gently to her from within her own mind.

'You must do what you do. There is no alternative. You are Wizardess of Canabria for good reason. Be yourself; follow what is in your heart!'

She waited for more, but there was none. While it was comforting to hear his voice, it was a small comfort, as she knew that to be herself meant to be a small girl and what was in her heart was fear and doubt.

Gradually she became aware of movement in the thick mist in front of her and then she heard the quiet squeaking of wooden wheels, the soft clumping of many hooves, the creaking of leather and the dull clanging of heavy metal. When the noises stopped, she smelled horses, grease, leather, wood and the unwashed bodies of an army of men excited for battle. Although she could see nothing, however much she strained her eyes, she knew that the Horsacks had arrived with their catapults and battering rams, stretched around the banks of the castle moat, waiting just beyond the curtain of fog. She felt suddenly very cold, a chill that came from within, freezing her to the spot.

Looking up, she saw that the sky was lightening and the mist was slowly rising with the dawn. Peering straight ahead, she saw a dark shape beginning to loom in the gloom in front of her and gradually she realized that it was the head of a Horsack horse. At this moment of recognition, the horse became aware of her. His eyes widened and his ears pricked up. He took a step forward and snorted the air to catch her scent. He shook his head in alarm, sending a ripple of surprise spreading through the other horses positioned at either side, before moving hurriedly back into the fog.

While the Horsack riders struggled to restrain and quiet their mounts, Jescinta became aware of movement behind her. Looking over her shoulder, she saw the dark shapes of wolves creeping along the bank of the moat, spreading out and lying low to the ground. She could smell their damp fur and so could the Horsack horses, who once again broke out into a chorus of snorting and nervous whinnies.

When it again fell quiet, Jescinta saw the horse emerge from the mist once more, urged on by his rider, the Horsack general. He leaned forward in his saddle, straining to see what had spooked his horse. Jescinta's cloak with its raised hood blended perfectly into the darkness, leaving only her face visible to the Horsack general.

For a long moment he stared at the white features of a frightened girl's face that seemed to hover disembodied in the fog. Her wide innocent eyes and helpless fear recalled to his mind all the battles he had fought, all the death and suffering he had seen, all the children he had orphaned and maimed, and he saw the faces of his own beloved children, his own daughter staring at him in fear and reproach.

"Ghost!" he gasped, pulling on his horse's reins to back into the darkness and escape from the vision of his guilt in the mist.

Upon hearing their general's frightened exclamation, confusion and fear spread along the Horsack lines, horses neighed and men shouted out, repeating the sighting of a ghost or calling for order. Jescinta, more frightened than ever, stood rooted, unable to move from her vulnerable position in front of an excited army she expected to fall upon her in a murderous frenzy. To her ever increasing horror, she saw a large black dog emerge from the noise and the fog to stand before her, growling, baring his fangs and preparing to pounce at her throat.

Just then, Lupus, the wolf-king stepped forward to stand beside her. He raised his head and opened his throat to fill the air with a dreadful howl that chilled the bones and silenced the nervous Horsacks. His pack rose up from their positions along the bank of the moat and added their voices to his, causing a new and greater panic to engulf the would-be invaders.

Then an even greater call came out from within the castle walls behind, a chant of a thousand voices booming and echoing in the gloom with drums pounding and horns blaring:

Allllsworrrthyyyy! Allllsworrrthyyyy!
All ye worthies! All ye worthies!
Arise and ride! Arise and ride!
Allllsworrrthyyyy! Allllsworrthyyyy!

Cries of alarm went up from the Horsack lines as they began to break up and retreat. Then the castle's great drawbridge crashed open and the Allsworthy cavalry thundered across, led by King Lufalot waving his sceptre in the air, followed by Marsad swinging his club and Sir Gawain brandishing his mighty sword. Then all the rest of the cavalry came, still chanting with Bartalemew, singing at the top of his lungs upon his ox, alongside all the commoners of the city with axes and pitchforks and whatever else they could find to defend their city.

The Horsacks fled in a blind panic, leaving behind their war machines, with the wolf pack close on their heels, nipping at the horses' hooves. Lupus remained by Jescinta's side, watching the black dog that still threatened the girl, as the Allsworthy army charged past in pursuit. Soon it fell quiet again as the battle disappeared into the dark, foggy forest.

Jescinta, as still as ever through all this, watched the black dog, who snarled, growled and threatened to pounce. His wide eyes glared with hatred at the girl who had foiled his plans but they also measured his chances against the wolf who stood beside her with hackles raised, ready to meet his charge. The dog seemed to come to a decision and it slowly rose up on its hind legs and became a man. There was no flash of light or puff of smoke, just a man where once there had been a dog. She recognized him as the Wizard Krael.

"Well, little wizardess," he said in a snarling growl. "May I congratulate you on a fine piece of magic. This battle is yours, but the war is not over."

"Krael, you should be ashamed of yourself," the girl declared, voicing both disapproval and pity. "A wizard of your talent using the poor Horsacks to further your dreams of power! You should know better!"

"How dare you scold me!" he snarled. "You are but a child and unfit to judge me, Krael, the greatest and most powerful of the wizards. Give yourself a couple hundred years of mastery of magic and perhaps then you will understand my claim to power!"

The girl stood shaking her head resolutely, thinking, 'Never, never.'

"Pfff. You are beneath my realm of thought," he sneered. "We shall meet again. Until then, pleasant dreams."

Then he vanished, no flash of light, no smoke, just nothing where once there had been an evil wizard.

Oo-oo-luf chose this moment to return, landing lightly on Jescinta's shoulder.

"I see you haven't yet moved from this spot, mistress Jescinta. After inviting the wolves to your little gathering, I stopped to join a few mice and voles for a spot of breakfast. I hope I'm not too late. I haven't missed anything, have I?" he asked in all innocence.

Jescinta giggled, reaching up with one hand to stroke the owl's feathers while extending the other to the head of the wolf-king, Lupus.

"Oh Oo-oo-luf, you funny bird," she said, smiling. "I'll tell you later."

Chapter 16

Time to go Home

Jescinta knelt down, her arm encircling the thick neck of the wolf-king. "Well, Lupus, what are your thoughts?" she asked.

Lupus cocked his head in the direction of the chase, his ears pricked to detect news beyond the girl's hearing.

"It sounds as if the pack has our uninvited guests well and truly on the run and your humans are close behind. I don't think we should expect too much trouble from the Horsacks for a while," he replied confidently.

"Good," Jescinta said, rising to her feet. "Lupus, you promised to help in whatever way you could and you have been as good as your word. We couldn't have managed without you. However shall I repay you?"

"You could some day explain what this was all about and who the devil was that strange dog-man we just encountered. I fear I shall never understand humans. And you could visit Wolves' Tor again to learn how to hunt mice or else I shall have no peace from the darling Lupia, who is determined that you should do so."

"I shall do both in good time," Jescinta promised. "But now, I think the wizardly thing to do would be to return to my oak. Farewell, Lupus, good hunting."

"Happy trails, Jescinta, Wizardess of Canabria," called out the wolf-king, as the girl walked away toward the still open drawbridge.

Passing through the great gate with the little owl on her shoulder hooting and pontificating, Jescinta moved into the cobblestone courtyard of what she thought was a deserted castle. As she reached the centre, however, she stopped when she noticed a little head poke around a doorway to look at her. It was the girl who was the first to join in the Dance of Life and she stepped out into full view. She held a kitchen knife in her little hand. Then from behind pillars and into archways and in windows appeared all the citizens of Allsworthy who were too young, old or frail to join in the chase, each armed with whatever they could find to fight to the finish if their King had failed against the Horsacks. Queen Beatrix stepped out onto a balcony with a dagger in her hand and her maids-in waiting either side of her. After a moment's silence, she set her weapon down and began to clap her hands and soon all the children, old men,women and invalids joined in, their faces beaming. Jescinta blushed, gave a little wave and hurried toward the stables.

After a little searching, she found the stall where Bartalemew had quartered the stag-king, Urun. She opened the half-door and he came forward, struggling to control the quivering fear he felt at being so long in the confines of the human-made cubicle.

"Mistress Jescinta, I am so glad to see you," the deer murmured.

"Urun, you poor dear, this has been such a trial for you," the girl said, stroking his muzzle and imagining how he felt cooped up in this human cell, hearing the terrible din of the Allsworthy cavalry charge and the ensuing mayhem as they and the howling wolves chased away the Horsack army.

She led Urun out into the courtyard and when the applause started up again she raised her hand to bring it to a halt, not wanting to cause the stag any more anxiety.

"It's time to go home now," she said when they reached the drawbridge. "You run on ahead and gather your wits. Have a nibble and a drink and I shall follow along behind. I'll sound my horn for you to collect me and we'll hurry home. Off you go now."

Urun didn't even reply before bounding across the drawbridge and the open pastures between the castle and the forest, so pleased was he to be free again.

"If you have no objection, I too, shall fly on ahead," Oo-oo-luf declared. "I am a bit tired after my night's exertions and I shall find a quiet place to nap. I'll join you later and you can give a full report then."

"Yes, of course," Jescinta replied and the little owl flew north towards the forest. She turned and waved at the Allsworthians who had remained behind. She walked across the drawbridge and headed across the dew-soaked pastures. She became aware of how weary she was herself. Perhaps she, too, would find a place to rest for the day and begin the journey home at nightfall.

When she reached the forest edge, it was beginning to grow light. She turned to look back to the castle, the heavy outline of which she could see through the rising fog. It was going to be a fine day. The strange rain cloud that oppressed the city when she first saw it from this point was gone now.

She was just going to turn into the woods when she heard the faint tinkling of a horse's harness, the clanging of armour and the heavy thudding of hooves that signalled an approaching rider. Her first thought was that she was being pursued by Horsacks and a jolt of fear went through her. But as the rider emerged from the mist, she saw that it was Sir Gawain, obviously following the trail she had left in the dewy grass. He waved with relief and smiled as he pulled up and dismounted.

"Mistress Jescinta," the knight said a little breathlessly. "I hurried back to see how you fared as soon as I was able. I am joyful that you are well."

"Yes, I am fine, Gawain. Thank you for your concern. I am sorry that I left without saying good-bye, but I thought it was time I was going."

"Oh, of course, my lady, no need to apologize. I understand. So long as you are safe. The battle has been won, there is no more to be done here."

"What will you do now, Gawain?" Jescinta asked.

"We shall stay a few days here in Allsworthy. I would like to consult with Marsad about his defenses and the training of his excellent cavalry," the knight replied, always the professional warrior. "Then we shall head west in search of people I have heard of in a remote land who worship Our Lord. I have reason to believe that they may have knowledge of that which I seek."

"Oh, I hope that, for your sake, you find your carpenter's cup."

"For my sake, I need only continue the quest. The finding is for the sake of others."

Just then they heard the sound of another rider approaching as Bartalemew arrived. He slipped off his ox and came forward, tugging his fringe and smiling broadly.

"M-my lady, I w-wanted-d-d to say g-good-bye," the boy said with only a little difficulty.

"I am glad Bart. I shall think of you and Gawain. I hope we meet again. I would love to hear the whole of the Song of Bartalemew."

"I shall sing of you everywhere," Bart replied faultlessly.

"I am so grateful to the both of you," Jescinta said. "How can I ever thank you for what you have done?"

"The memory of you is thanks enough," Gawain said as he went down on one knee, took her hand and kissed it. Jescinta felt herself blush and she couldn't help but giggle and roll her eyes.

The two seekers swung up onto their mounts and headed back toward the Castle Allsworthy with a wave and the wizardess made her way into the forest.

Eventually Jescinta came to the spot by the stream where she and her party had met the heron Blue only the day before. She squatted to quench her thirst at the water's edge and was startled to hear a voice address her.

"I hope the drink was as refreshing as it was deserved," the voice said, seeming to come from a stick stuck in the shallows of the stream. The stick was, in fact, a great heron.

"Blue!" Jescinta exclaimed. "I'm so glad to see you. I feared you had fallen in the brave diversion you created to get us into Allsworthy."

"I was spared, mistress. Sadly, some of my feathered folk were not," Blue replied. "The important thing is that those dreadful humans are gone and we are safe to fly about our business and the frogs think they are safe to hop about theirs. I just wanted to thank you for meeting my great expectations of you and say farewell until our next meeting. Farewell, mistress Jescinta," he said, suddenly in a hurry.

"Good hunting, Blue," the girl called out as the heron's great wings carried him away. She was somewhat unsettled by his hurried good-by. What Jescinta didn't know was that Blue had seen that someone else wanted to speak to her.

"It went well, then?" a deep voice asked from behind.

She whirled around to look up into the bright green eyes of Goddell.

"Goddell, you are here! Where have you been?" Jescinta asked stupidly.

"I am so pleased you found a solution," the wizard said, ignoring the girl's confused question.

"Who told you?" Jescinta demanded to know. She shook herself, trying to be sensible. She should know by now, she thought to herself, to expect the unexpected from Goddell, but he always caught her out. He lived easily in the world of magic, and magic always catches you, leaves you stupefied and bewildered, breaking rules of expectation and logic, or else it wouldn't be magic.

"I assumed as much," Goddell replied.

"Yes, of course," Jescinta said, trying to gather herself and sound intelligent. "Well, yes, it did go well, I think. Goddell, it was Krael, he was behind it all!"

"So I understand, now," he said, looking down and giving a little shake of his head. His face betrayed concern, as if he was aware of problems beyond the girl's reckoning. He looked up and held her eyes with his. "It will have to be sorted out."

They stood looking into each other, their wizard minds racing through all the possibilities and impossibilities and beyond, like wizards do.

"But, for now, peace reigns again in Canabria," Goddell finally remarked, smiling at the girl. "All thanks to you. I am so proud of you."

Jescinta blushed and shrugged her shoulders before she explained that many others had played their part in the victory.

"I was going to rest here, beneath that willow. Can you join me?" she asked, hoping her voice didn't betray a note of pleading.

"Yes, that would be nice," Goddell replied.

They moved through the curtain of the tree's weeping limbs and settled themselves against its trunk. Goddell closed his eyes and seemed to sleep at once. Jescinta thought that her master must have been very busy for a very long time to be so tired, and she wondered what he had been up to since she last saw him at her tree home. She became suddenly aware of her own fatigue, the build-up of days of travel, adventure, excitement, danger, and magic. She closed her eyes and just as she felt a deep slumber creep over her, she remembered Krael's last words to her.

The thought shocked her to a frightened wakefulness. What nightmares did the twisted, old wizard intend for her? Was he going to intrude upon her sleeping mind to torment her when she was least aware, never letting her rest?

She looked at the master wizard asleep next to her. He seemed as if he was a part of the tree he slept against. No, she was safe here, now and for as long as she remembered him. Jescinta leaned over, settling her head on Goddell's lap, and she slept the sleep of a child.